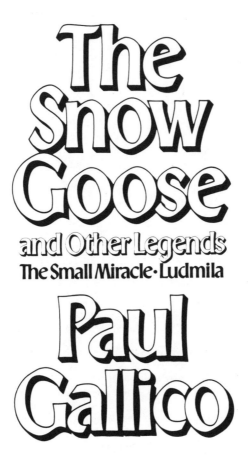

The Snow Goose

and Other Legends
The Small Miracle · Ludmila

Paul Gallico

D0169621

A WALLABY BOOK
PUBLISHED BY POCKET BOOKS NEW YORK

POCKET BOOKS, a Simon & Schuster division of
GULF & WESTERN CORPORATION
1230 Avenue of the Americas, New York, N.Y. 10020

"The Snow Goose" copyright 1940 by The Curtis Publishing Company
"The Small Miracle" ("Never Take No for an Answer") copyright
1950 by Paul Gallico; copyright 1952 by Doubleday & Company, Inc.
"Ludmila" copyright © 1959 by Doubleday & Company, Inc.

Published by arrangement with Doubleday & Company, Inc.

All rights reserved, including the right to reproduce
this book or portions thereof in any form whatsoever.
For information address Doubleday & Company, Inc.,
245 Park Avenue, New York, N.Y. 10017

ISBN: 0-671-79055-2

First Wallaby printing November, 1978

10 9 8 7 6 5 4 3 2 1

Trademarks registered in the United States and other countries.

Printed in the U.S.A.

CONTENTS

The Snow Goose
and Other Legends
The Small Miracle · Ludmila

INTRODUCTION

The Stories behind the Legends

IT might be considered impertinent to assume that any reader would be interested in the stories behind the three legends presented in this volume, except for the fact that they have an unusual feature in common. All three of them originated as short stories appearing in magazines; all three of them later became books. And each has an animal as a central figure as well as humans: a cow, a donkey and a bird.

Yet it was not the animals that inspired these three tales. It would be more truthful to say that they came into being because of affection for all animals but in particular for a people, a Saint and a country.

I lived once for seven years on the mountainside in the tiny principality of Liechtenstein and yet only once used it as the background for a story, when the London magazine *The Sketch,* in 1953 commissioned me to write them a story for their Christmas issue, and I chose then to invent the miracle of the underprivileged little cow who found a mysterious weed in a hidden valley and became a success.

Yet the cow was incidental to the innocence of the wayside shrine of the Madonna in her coffin-shaped shelter beneath the rocks on the mountain road from Steg up to the high alpine pastures at Malbun, where the peasants took their cattle for the summer months.

The peasants too are innocent, brutal but naive and if the country priests were sometimes a little shabby and not entirely free of guile their belief too confirmed their innocence. They were believers, these were all believers, even the chief herdsman who so proudly wore his disbelief perhaps was the strongest believer of them all. In a land and in a community where there is belief, miracles would seem to be possible.

There is a curious fact that none of these three stories was written either in or even close to where they take place. *The Snow Goose,* set on the Essex coast, was written in San Francisco; *The Small Miracle,* which takes place in Assisi, was written in New York and *Ludmila,* a story of the high Liechtenstein Alps, was composed in Tel Aviv, where I was visiting.

On the whole I think this was all to the good. Distance lends not only enchantment but perspective and makes selection simpler. Those things about a place which remain most vividly in your mind when you are away from them are quite likely to be the most important and the most picturesque. No one who has ever seen the taupe-colored cows descending from the high pastures of Liechtenstein to the valley, decked out in their finery of colored ribbons, their milking stools tied between their horns, gay with flowers and rosettes as well as sacred symbols, can ever forget it or fail to be touched by it. Again it is the innocence of it all that is so moving. The symbols are Christian but the innocence is pagan.

Ludmila is purely and simply a fairytale from a fairytale land. Though the valley bottom, where courses the Rhine and Vaduz, the capital, nestles, is sophisticated and cynical, a nest of lawyers and hypocrites, that region above the cloud level that often darkens the length of the land while 4,000 feet above the sun shines on the peaks, that portion of the Alps with snow cliffs and deep clefts is the home of legend. Werewolves still roam, witches fly, kobolds mine and little people dance. The high herdsmen see and hear things that those from the valley are not privileged to share.

There is no help for it but the things that take place in this wild, rugged country must appear supernatural. Streams undermine the rocks, small furry things rustle unseen through the underbrush, passing clouds cast weird shadows or descend sometimes to blot out the peaks and fill the dark gorges with impenetrable mists. The whirr of heavy wings at dawn and the shadow cast by great pinions could be a passing eagle—or an angel. The people who live close to a nature of such formidable proportions are less inclined to be skeptical of matters which seem to be beyond their ken. The task of the priests was not too difficult; they had merely to translate the marvelous into the miraculous. Things seemingly inexplicable happening on the heights and hence that much closer to the sky were easily ascribed to manifestations of the hand of God, or if necessary to God's arch-enemy.

The mountain people are primitive, primordial and atavistic and not greatly altered by modern times. The problems of the high pastures have remained unchanged since ancient days and the people who cope with them are not much different either. Most of their customs and habits come from something so old their origin is lost. They are as old if not older than the Roman markers and bits of stonework scattered throughout the mountains. The garlanding and bedecking of the cows for their autumn descent stems surely from some pagan harvest festival. If it is romance you ever come seeking in Liechtenstein you must not look for it in the valley below, but instead search the glens and grottoes of the Bettlerjoch or come in spring to see the pale crocuses carpet the high valley of Steg.

There is a horror story locked away in that area of superstition, greed and untold human misery cast by the accusation of witchcraft and as recently as a few years ago some families still remained under a curse visited upon unborn generations. And other living legends of Liechtenstein are grim reminders of ages of black magic, erring maidens turned to stone and punishments visited upon lovers. *Ludmila* is a gentler tale but compounded of the same elements and when I am asked "Did it really happen?", I can only say that since the story took place a hundred years ago, which was before I was born, I do not know. But it *could* have happened.

The Small Miracle grew out of a visit to the tomb of St. Francis in his crypt in the church at Assisi. It was not in any sense a pilgrimage but a passing through. Yet the fact remains that when I left Assisi with clouds from the dusty road rising behind my car, I was not the same as I had been a few hours before climbing the hill to the city crowning it. I had been moved emotionally.

It was the simplicity of his tomb that had reached to my heart, a small chamber, a plain sarcophagus, a shaft of light slanting from the sky to fall upon it, as though the heavens were spotlighting the last resting-place of a favorite son.

Such had been the innocence and modesty of the man that his church had apparently found it impossible to descend to those usual lapses of taste connected with the graves and relics of its Saints; gold, silver, precious stones and trumpery. They were permitting Francis to sleep as he had lived.

Until this visit my knowledge of Francis of Assisi was

10

limited, barren and certainly incomplete. I had never read a life or a biography; I did not even know what had impelled him suddenly to a life of austerity and sacrifice. Yet standing there in the crypt I seemed to feel his presence and thought I could hear some of the singing that once arose from his heart. Later, when I emerged once more into the daylight, he was there and I had the feeling that any moment when I turned a corner I might find him preaching in the square, for the cobbles that he had trodden were still under foot and the old streets and plazas and churches had changed very little since his time.

Thereafter I read avidly about him and loved him for his courage and his simplicity and I suspect envied him too. I remember with what enchantment I read that when some rich man left money at his door in place of the stones and mortar Francis had begged to build his church, the Saint consigned the cash to the dung heap where, in his estimation, it belonged. His humor was forthright, Italian and mischievous. He seemed to be the only Saint I ever read about who could laugh.

I felt impelled to write about him. I wanted to recreate him, to free him from his stone prison in the dark chamber and set him to striding the slanted streets of Assisi once more. This was neither ambition nor arrogance but merely devotion and since I aimed at doing this in a short story, presumptuous and probably impossible. That it turned out to be a story of a small boy who owned a donkey and wished to beg a miracle from the little heap of bones and dust locked in the coffin, is yet another example of the writer being subject to his own creation. The story was written in 1950 and published in *Good Housekeeping* magazine under the title *Never Take No for an Answer*.

A short story is usually an ephemeral thing which at

best can hope for survival in some anthology, but every so often one will assume a life of its own and fare forth to make its way in the world as a little book. I should say I have been extraordinarily lucky in that all three of the tales contained in this volume escaped from the magazines in which they were first printed.

Never Take No for an Answer acquired two lives, one as the book first published by Michael Joseph Ltd. of London and Doubleday of New York under the title *The Small Miracle* and the other as an unpretentious little British film made by producer Anthony Havelock-Allan and screened under the title *Never Take No.*

Why all these changes in title? *Never Take No for an Answer* was considered intriguing for *Good House-keeping* and *The Small Miracle,* the best of all the titles, described the book exactly. For some reason or other the film trade shied away from the "miracle" and compromised on the not too happy title of *Never Take No.* The film was notable for having been photographed on two of the most expensive sets in the entire history of motion picture production. For the basilica of St. Francis in Assisi and the Vatican in Rome were placed at our disposal. Lights, props, cameras, directors, actors, boy and donkey were welcomed within its sacred walls.

The strangest things happened in connection with the picture. The boy actor who played Pepino we discovered in the drawing-room of Lady Berkeley, then living in Assisi. He was an Italian war orphan she had adopted. He never made another picture but was educated in England and is now an English gentleman. The donkey, Violetta, when the picture was finished became star-struck and refused to work and the last time I saw her she was as fat and lazy as an alderman. One of the Vatican guards was played by an old friend of mine from a former life that I had led in the long ago. His name was Enzo

Fiermonte, one-time challenger for the light-heavyweight boxing title, which brought back memories of the last time I had seen him as I sat with my nose up against the ring floor in Madison Square Garden watching him being abused by a character flourishing under the name of Slapsie Maxie Rosenbloom. It was a bad night for the Proud Mountain and shortly after he retired from the ring. The film cut no great swath but every so often around Easter or Christmas it is still revived or seen on television. And this book too seems to have survived and in its small way accomplished what I asked of it, that it should remind us in these beastly, selfish, material times that there once was a man strong, utterly noble and self-sacrificing in his faith in and love of God.

The story behind the story of *The Snow Goose* happened so long ago, twenty-three years to be exact, almost a quarter of a century and I am almost distrustful of my memory on detail but of its genesis I have no doubt; I can remember it as strongly and clearly as though it were yesterday. I was thrilled to the core by the British evacuation of Dunkirk and felt that I wished to make a song about it. Felt is almost too mild a word, it was a need, a yearning and almost a compulsion. The human courage, the indomitable human spirit of the men who put forth from Britain in every kind of small craft to rescue their own from the beaches sang inside of me like the peal of an organ. I wished I had been a composer to release the melody or failing that a poet, and being neither I did the best I could with the tools of my profession; I wrote a short story. I was living in San Francisco at the time, simply from choice for it is one of the most exciting cities of the world. One of the advantages of being a writer is that one is tied to no place and no city. Your office is where you hang your hat. I heard and read so much about San Francisco, in the early spring of 1940 I went there.

The war was on and like millions of Americans I followed the fortunes of the British but mine was something of a special interest, for I owned one tiny little morsel of England. In 1936 I had bought a small house and garden on a hillside on the Devon coast, overlooking the sea.

The cold war came to an end, the Germans drove to the sea and the British set out in their small boats by the hundreds to spirit their defeated army off the beaches of Dunkirk.

Where do short stories come from? Often enough out of an emotion as the mainspring, but thereafter the feeling must be clothed and presented. And from this point many things take over, the subconscious, old memories, etc. In the library of my rented flat atop Nob Hill in San Francisco was a set of Kipling and I had just been reading *Soldiers Three*. The men on the beaches would not have been much different from those of Kipling's day. Soldiers were alike in every generation. But mostly my mind seemed to turn to a friend, Peter Scott, whom I had met in London several years before. The son of Scott of the Antarctic, Peter lived in an abandoned lighthouse on the Essex coast which was a wildfowl sanctuary. Here he studied, read about and painted the wild birds passing through. Too, Peter was a small boat sailor and used to take part in races at Cowes and Kiel. If he was not already in the Navy I knew that Peter would have been a part of that flotilla which had set out to save the Army. I had seen the snow geese at Peter's sanctuary and heard him tell of the mystery of these birds who would return each year, dropping out of the sky like visiting angels and somehow Dunkirk and the snow geese and a bird painter and *Soldiers Three* began to become

14

inextricably entangled in my mind. And the little girl who came to the lighthouse with the injured goose—I don't know who she was or where she came from, except perhaps out of that part of my subconscious which had always yearned for the daughter I had never had. All of these went into the hopper and out of it came a short story of 8,000 words called *The Snow Goose,* which was submitted to *The Saturday Evening Post* and promptly rejected by them.

Since I was then already an established *Post* writer this was a good example of the fallacy that once one had a name one could sell anything. It might also serve as an object lesson to young writers. Nothing is ever accepted because of a reputation. The greater the reputation the more difficult are the editors. Every story is judged upon its merits.

The complaint against the original version of *The Snow Goose* was that my hero, the deformed painter and the girl Fritha, now grown into woman, had fallen in love and she had come to live with him at his lighthouse before his departure to France, from which he was never to return. At the time I was writing the story it seemed to me a natural thing to happen to these two people and to add poignancy and drama to the final tragedy. The viewpoint of the editors was that their readers would not like to see a man with a deformity united to a healthy girl. *The Saturday Evening Post,* it must be remembered, was then a family magazine published for Americans and hence subject to all kinds of odd taboos. What was interesting about this particular one was that it was not the living together to which they objected, but the fact that the man was a hunchback.

They might have been wrong and they might have been very right. In fact the subsequent history of this story and its success would indicate that in all probability

15

their criticism was valid. I remember at the time I received it I was upset and angry. I didn't want anyone tampering with my story. I thought that a love which could look beyond the outer shell to the spirit within was the better love than the usual formula infatuation of the girl for the handsome boy.

Yes, except for this one point, they were satisfied with the story and had not complained about the unhappy ending. I thought it over for a week, cooled down and rewrote it so that Rhayader departed from Fritha before their love had been consummated.

The story appeared in *The Post* and a year later as a slim volume, published by Alfred Knopf in New York.

The Snow Goose then developed into a publishing freak, one of those occasional literary accidents for which neither author nor publisher can be held responsible, or take credit. It is a once in a lifetime happening for a writer. For twenty years I have been giving lame answers to the question "When are you going to write another *Snow Goose?*"

The Snow Goose journeyed to England with a packet of material sent by Knopf during the war to Michael Joseph Ltd. Again the little book came close to not being published. The late Michael Joseph, for many years my friend, adviser and guide to my British public, himself told me the story. He was a soldier then and in camp somewhere in Britain, preparing to go overseas, when he received *The Snow Goose* from his office among other items. But to *The Snow Goose* was attached a note, "We don't want to publish this, do we? Too short!"

Michael told me that he read it through at a sitting and felt that the office criticism of the slim volume was one of its virtues. There was a war on; paper was scarce; and the sands of time were running out more quickly; brevity was no handicap. He wrote back to say that they were to publish it. *The Snow Goose* began its career in Great Britain.

Later, when the book had established itself, Michael Joseph published an illustrated edition and a more apt and felicitous illustrator could not have been chosen. It was Peter Scott, who, with his own career and writings on wildfowl and his paintings and his lighthouse, had been a part of the inspiration for the story. Beyond these features, of course, there was no connection and no resemblance of any kind between Peter and Rhayader, for the person and character of the painter is wholly fictional as is the story itself, though I am told that in some quarters the snow goose appearing over Dunkirk has been accepted as legend and I have been compelled to reply to many correspondents that it was sheer invention.

The Snow Goose has had many adventures in the film world. It was first acquired by the late Gabriel Pascal, producer of *Pygmalion, Major Barbara* and *Caesar and Cleopatra* and later owned by J. Arthur Rank and assigned to David Lean to film. But the *ad valorem* tax on films cropped up just then; it was never made and the rights have reverted to me. Since then many producers have discussed the turning of this story into a film, but none to any purpose. For this single story has made me many friends in Britain and I would be more than ungrateful were I to permit this story to be Hollywoodized, or changed beyond recognition by producers who are frustrated writers, or writers who are themselves no writers and get their kicks out of altering the work of others.

This, then, is how these stories came about and here are the tales themselves. I was amused to look back and note that *The Snow Goose* was copyrighted in 1940, *The Small Miracle* in 1950, and *Ludmila* in 1959, the stories spanning thirty years and oddly, at ten-year intervals. Thus, here in America a whole, new generation has grown up that has never seen them before. Whether they have withstood this drastic test of time must be for you to judge.

Paul Gallico

The Snow Goose
and Other Legends
The Small Miracle · Ludmila

The Snow Goose

THE Great Marsh lies on the Essex coast between the village of Chelmbury and the ancient Saxon oyster-fishing hamlet of Wickaeldroth. It is one of the last of the wild places of England, a low, far-reaching expanse of grass and reeds and half-submerged meadowlands ending in the great saltings and mud flats and tidal pools near the restless sea.

Tidal creeks and estuaries and the crooked, meandering arms of many little rivers whose mouths lap at the edge of the ocean cut through the sodden land that seems to rise and fall and breathe with the recurrence of the daily tides. It is desolate, utterly lonely, and made lonelier by the calls and cries of the wildfowl that make their homes in the marshlands and saltings—the wild-geese and the gulls, the teal and widgeon, the redshanks and curlews that pick their way through the tidal pools. Of human habitants there are none, and none are seen, with the occasional exception of a wild-fowler or native oyster-fishermen, who still ply a trade already ancient when the Normans came to Hastings.

Grays and blues and soft greens are the colors, for when the skies are dark in the long winters, the many waters of the beaches and marshes reflect the cold and somber color. But sometimes, with sunrise and sunset, sky and land are aflame with red and golden fire.

Hard by one of the winding arms of the little River Aelder runs the embankment of an old sea wall, smooth and solid, without a break, a bulwark to the land against the encroaching sea. Deep into a salting some three miles from the North Sea it runs, and there turns north. At that corner its face is gouged, broken, and shattered. It has been breached, and at the breach the hungry sea has already entered and taken for its own the land, the wall, and all that stood there.

At low water the blackened and ruptured stones of the ruins of an abandoned lighthouse show above the surface, with here and there, like buoy markers, the top of a sagging fence post. Once this lighthouse abutted on the sea and was a beacon on the Essex coast. Time shifted land and water, and its usefulness came to an end.

Lately it served again as a human habitation. In it there lived a lonely man. His body was warped, but his heart was filled with love for wild and hunted things. He was ugly to look upon, but he created great beauty. It is about him, and a child who came to know him and see beyond the grotesque form that housed him to what lay within, that this story is told.

It is not a story that falls easily and smoothly into sequence. It had been garnered from many sources and from many people. Some of it comes in the form of fragments from men who looked upon strange and violent scenes. For the sea has claimed its own and spreads its rippled blanket over the site, and the great white bird with the black-tipped pinions that saw it all from the beginning to the end has returned to the dark, frozen silences of the northlands whence it came.

In the late spring of 1930 Philip Rhayader came to the abandoned lighthouse at the mouth of the Aelder. He bought the light and many acres of marshland and salting surrounding it.

He lived and worked there alone the year round. He was a painter of birds and of nature, who, for reasons, had withdrawn from all human society. Some of the reasons were apparent on his fortnightly visits to the little village of Chelmbury for supplies, where the natives looked askance at his misshapen body and dark visage. For he was a hunchback and his left arm was crippled, thin and bent at the wrist, like the claw of a bird.

They soon became used to his queer figure, small but powerful, the massive, dark, bearded head set just slightly below the mysterious mound on his back, the glowing eyes and the clawed hand, and marked him off as "that queer painter chap that lives down to lighthouse."

Physical deformity often breeds hatred of humanity in men. Rhayader did not hate; he loved very greatly, man, the animal kingdom, and all nature. His heart was filled with pity and understanding. He had mastered his handicap, but he could not master the rebuffs he suffered, due to his appearance. The thing that drove him into seclusion was his failure to find anywhere a return of the warmth that flowed from him. He repelled women. Men would have warmed to him had they got to know him. But the mere fact that an effort was being made hurt Rhayader and drove him to avoid the person making it.

He was twenty-seven when he came to the Great Marsh. He had traveled much and fought valiantly before he made the decision to withdraw from a world in which he could not take part as other men. For all of the artist's sensitivity and woman's tenderness locked in his barrel breast, he was very much a man.

In his retreat he had his birds, his painting, and his

boat. He owned a sixteen-footer, which he sailed with wonderful skill. Alone, with no eyes to watch him, he managed well with his deformed hand, and he often used his strong teeth to handle the sheets of his billowing sails in a tricky blow.

He would sail the tidal creeks and estuaries and out to sea, and would be gone for days at a time, looking for new species of birds to photograph or sketch, and he became an adept at netting them to add to his collection of tamed wildfowl in the pen near his studio that formed the nucleus of a sanctuary.

He never shot over a bird, and wild-fowlers were not welcome near his premises. He was a friend to all things wild, and the wild things repaid him with their friendship.

Tamed in his enclosures were the geese that came winding down the coast from Iceland and Spitsbergen each October, in great skeins that darkened the sky and filled the air with the rushing noise of their passage—the brown-bodied pink-feet, white-breasted barnacles with their dark necks and clowns' masks, the wild white fronts with black-barred breasts, and many species of wild ducks—widgeon, mallard, pintails, teal, and shovelers.

Some were pinioned, so that they would remain there as a sign and signal to the wild ones that came down at each winter's beginning that here were food and sanctuary.

Many hundreds came and remained with him all through the cold weather from October to the early spring, when they migrated north again to their breeding-grounds below the ice rim.

Rhayader was content in the knowledge that when storms blew, or it was bitter cold and food was scarce, or the big punt guns of the distant bag hunters roared, his birds were safe; that he had gathered to the sanctuary and security of his own arms and heart these many wild and beautiful creatures who knew and trusted him.

They would answer the call of the north in the spring, but in the fall they would come back, barking and whooping and honking in the autumn sky, to circle the landmark of the old light and drop to earth near by to be his guests again—birds that he well remembered and recognized from the previous year.

And this made Rhayader happy, because he knew that implanted somewhere in their beings was the germ knowledge of his existence and his safe haven, that this knowledge had become a part of them and, with the coming of the gray skies and the winds from the north, would send them unerringly back to him.

For the rest, his heart and soul went into the painting of the country in which he lived and its creatures. There are not many Rhayaders extant. He hoarded them jealously, piling them up in his lighthouse and the storerooms above by the hundreds. He was not satisfied with them, because as an artist he was uncompromising.

But the few that have reached the market are masterpieces, filled with the glow and colors of marsh-reflected light, the feel of flight, the push of birds breasting a morning wind bending the tall flag reeds. He painted the loneliness and the smell of the salt-laden cold, the eternity and agelessness of marshes, the wild, living creatures, dawn flights, and frightened things taking to the air, and winged shadows at night hiding from the moon.

One November afternoon, three years after Rhayader had come to the Great Marsh, a child approached the lighthouse studio by means of the sea wall. In her arms she carried a burden.

She was no more than twelve, slender, dirty, nervous and timid as a bird, but beneath the grime as eerily beautiful as a marsh fairy. She was pure Saxon, large-boned, fair, with a head to which her body was yet to grow, and deep-set, violet-colored eyes.

She was desperately frightened of the ugly man she had come to see, for legend had already begun to gather about Rhayader, and the native wild-fowlers hated him for interfering with their sport.

But greater than her fear was the need of that which she bore. For locked in her child's heart was the knowledge, picked up somewhere in the swampland, that this ogre who lived in the lighthouse had magic that could heal injured things.

She had never seen Rhayader before and was close to fleeing in panic at the dark apparition that appeared at the studio door, drawn by her footsteps—the black head and beard, the sinister hump, and the crooked claw.

She stood there staring, poised like a disturbed marsh bird for instant flight.

But his voice was deep and kind when he spoke to her. "What is it, child?"

She stood her ground, and then edged timidly forward. The thing she carried in her arms was a large white bird, and it was quite still. There were stains of blood on its whiteness and on her kirtle where she had held it to her.

The girl placed it in his arms. "I found it, sir. It's hurted. Is it still alive?"

"Yes. Yes, I think so. Come in, child, come in."

Rhayader went inside, bearing the bird, which he placed upon a table, where it moved feebly. Curiosity overcame fear. The girl followed and found herself in a room warmed by a coal fire, shining with many colored pictures that covered the walls, and full of a strange but pleasant smell.

The bird fluttered. With his good hand Rhayader

spread one of its immense white pinions. The end was beautifully tipped with black.

Rhayader looked and marveled, and said: "Child, where did you find it?"

"In t' marsh, sir, where fowlers had been. What—what is it, sir?"

"It's a snow goose from Canada. But how in all heaven came it here?"

The name seemed to mean nothing to the little girl. Her deep violet eyes, shining out of the dirt on her thin face, were fixed with concern on the injured bird.

She said: "Can 'ee heal it, sir?"

"Yes, yes," said Rhayader. "We will try. Come, you shall help me."

There were scissors and bandages and splints on a shelf, and he was marvelously deft, even with the crooked claw that managed to hold things.

He said: "Ah, she has been shot, poor thing. Her leg is broken, and the wing tip, but not badly. See, we will clip her primaries, so that we can bandage it, but in the spring the feathers will grow and she will be able to fly again. We'll bandage it close to her body, so that she cannot move it until it has set, and then make a splint for the poor leg."

Her fears forgotten, the child watched, fascinated, as he worked, and all the more so because while he fixed a fine splint to the shattered leg he told her the most wonderful story.

The bird was a young one, no more than a year old. She was born in a northern land far, far across the seas, a land belonging to England. Flying to the south to escape the snow and ice and bitter cold, a great storm had seized her and whirled and buffeted her about. It was a truly terrible storm, stronger than her great wings, stronger than anything. For days and nights it held her in its grip and there was nothing she could do but fly before it. When finally it had blown itself out and her sure instincts took her south again, she was over a different land and surrounded by strange birds that she had never seen before. At last, exhausted by her ordeal, she had sunk to rest in a friendly green marsh, only to be met by the blast from the hunter's gun.

"A bitter reception for a visiting princess," concluded Rhayader. "We will call her *'La Princesse Perdue,'* the Lost Princess. And in a few days she will be feeling much better. See?" He reached into his pocket and produced a handful of grain. The snow goose opened its round yellow eyes and nibbled at it.

The child laughed with delight, and then suddenly caught her breath with alarm as the full import of where she was pressed in upon her, and without a word she turned and fled out of the door.

"Wait, wait!" cried Rhayader, and went to the entrance, where he stopped so that it framed his dark bulk. The girl was already fleeing down the sea wall, but she paused at his voice and looked back.

"What is your name, child?"

"Frith."

"Eh?" said Rhayader. "Fritha, I suppose. Where do you live?"

"Wi' t' fisherfolk at Wickaeldroth." She gave the name the old Saxon pronunciation.

"Will you come back tomorrow, or the next day, to see how the Princess is getting along?"

She paused, and again Rhayader must have thought of the wild water birds caught motionless in that split second of alarm before they took to flight.

But her thin voice came back to him: "Ay!"

And then she was gone, with her fair hair streaming out behind her.

The snow goose mended rapidly and by midwinter was already limping about the enclosure with the wild pink-footed geese with which it associated, rather than the barnacles, and had learned to come to be fed at Rhayader's call. And the child, Fritha, or Frith, was a frequent visitor. She had overcome her fear of Rhayader. Her imagination was captured by the presence of this strange white princess from a land far over the sea, a land that was all pink, as she knew from the map that Rhayader showed her, and on which they traced the stormy path of the lost bird from its home in Canada to the Great Marsh of Essex.

Then one June morning a group of late pink-feet, fat and well fed from the winter at the lighthouse, answered the stronger call of the breeding-grounds and rose lazily, climbing into the sky in ever widening circles. With them, her white body and black-tipped pinions shining in the spring sun, was the snow goose. It so happened that Frith was at the lighthouse. Her cry brought Rhayader running from the studio.

"Look! Look! The Princess! Be she going away?"

Rhayader stared into the sky at the climbing specks. "Ay," he said, unconsciously dropping into her manner of speech. "The Princess is going home. Listen! She is bidding us farewell."

Out of the clear sky came the mournful barking of the pink-feet, and above it the higher, clearer note of the snow goose. The specks drifted northward, formed into a tiny *V*, diminished, and vanished.

With the departure of the snow goose ended the visits of Frith to the lighthouse. Rhayader learned all over again the meaning of the word "loneliness." That summer, out of his memory, he painted a picture of a slender, grime-covered child, her fair hair blown by a November storm, who bore in her arms a wounded white bird.

In mid-October the miracle occurred. Rhayader was in his enclosure, feeding his birds. A gray northeast wind was blowing and the land was sighing beneath the incoming tide. Above the sea and the wind noises he heard a clear, high note. He turned his eyes upward to the evening sky in time to see first an infinite speck, then a black-and-white-pinioned dream that circled the lighthouse once, and finally a reality that dropped to earth in the pen and came waddling forward importantly to be fed, as though she had never been away. It was the snow goose. There was no mistaking her. Tears of joy came to Rhayader's eyes. Where had she been? Surely not home to Canada. No, she must have summered in Greenland or Spitsbergen with the pink-feet. She had remembered and had returned.

When next Rhayader went in to Chelmbury for supplies, he left a message with the postmistress—one that must have caused her much bewilderment. He said: "Tell Frith, who lives with the fisherfolk at Wickaeldroth, that the Lost Princess has returned."

Three days later, Frith, taller, still tousled and unkempt, came shyly to the lighthouse to visit La Princesse Perdue.

Time passed. On the Great Marsh it was marked by the height of the tides, the slow march of the seasons, the passage of the birds, and, for Rhayader, by the arrival and departure of the snow goose.

The world outside boiled and seethed and rumbled with the eruption that was soon to break forth and come close to marking its destruction. But not yet did it touch upon Rhayader, or, for that matter, Frith. They had fallen into a curious, natural rhythm, even as the child grew older. When the snow goose was at the lighthouse, then she came, too, to visit and learn many things from Rhayader. They sailed together in his speedy boat, that he handled so skillfully. They caught wild fowl for the ever increasing colony, and built new pens and enclosures for them. From him she learned the lore of every wild bird, from gull to gyrfalcon, that flew the marshes. She cooked for him sometimes, and even learned to mix his paints.

But when the snow goose returned to its summer home, it was as though some kind of bar was up between them, and she did not come to the lighthouse. One year the bird did not return, and Rhayader was heartbroken. All things seemed to have ended for him. He painted furiously through the winter and the next summer, and never once saw the child. But in the fall the familiar cry once more rang from the sky, and the huge white bird, now at its full growth, dropped from the skies as mysteriously as it had departed. Joyously, Rhayader sailed his boat into Chelmbury and left his message with the postmistress.

Curiously, it was more than a month after he had left the message before Frith reappeared at the lighthouse, and Rhayader, with a shock, realized that she was a child no longer.

After the year in which the bird had remained away, its periods of absence grew shorter and shorter. It had grown so tame that it followed Rhayader about and even came into the studio while he was working.

In the spring of 1940 the birds migrated early from the Great Marsh. The world was on fire. The whine and roar of the bombers and the thudding explosions frightened them. The first day of May, Frith and Rhayader stood shoulder to shoulder on the sea wall and watched the last of the unpinioned pink-feet and barnacle geese rise from their sanctuary; she, tall, slender, free as air, and hauntingly beautiful; he, dark, grotesque, his massive bearded head raised to the sky, his glowing dark eyes watching the geese form their flight tracery.

"Look, Philip," Frith said.

Rhayader followed her eyes. The snow goose had taken flight, her giant wings spread, but she was flying low, and once came quite close to them, so that for a moment the spreading black-tipped, white pinions seemed to caress them and they felt the rush of the bird's swift passage. Once, twice, she circled the lighthouse, then dropped to earth again in the enclosure with the pinioned geese and commenced to feed.

"She be'ent going," said Frith, with marvel in her voice. The bird in its close passage seemed to have woven a kind of magic about her. "The Princess be goin' t' stay."

"Ay," said Rhayader, and his voice was shaken too. "She'll stay. She will never go away again. The Lost Princess is lost no more. This is her home now—of her own free will."

The spell the bird had girt about her was broken, and Frith was suddenly conscious of the fact that she was frightened, and the things that frightened her were in Rhayader's eyes—the longing and the loneliness and the deep, welling, unspoken things that lay in and behind them as he turned them upon her.

His last words were repeating themselves in her head as though he had said them again: "This is her home now—of her own free will." The delicate tendrils of her instincts reached to him and carried to her the message of the things he could not speak because of what he felt himself to be, misshapen and grotesque. And where his voice might have soothed her, her fright grew greater at his silence and the power of the unspoken things between them. The woman in her bade her take flight from something that she was not yet capable of understanding.

Frith said: "I—I must go. Good-by. I be glad the—the Princess will stay. You'll not be so alone now."

She turned and walked swiftly away, and his sadly spoken "Good-by, Frith," was only a half-heard ghost of a sound borne to her ears above the rustling of the marsh grass. She was far away before she dared turn for a backward glance. He was still standing on the sea wall, a dark speck against the sky.

Her fear had stilled now. It had been replaced by something else, a queer sense of loss that made her stand quite still for a moment, so sharp was it. Then, more slowly, she continued on, away from the skyward-pointing finger of the lighthouse and the man beneath it.

It was a little more than three weeks before Frith returned to the lighthouse. May was at its end, and the day, too, in a long golden twilight that was giving way to the silver of the moon already hanging in the eastern sky.

She told herself, as her steps took her thither, that she must know whether the snow goose had really stayed, as Rhayader said it would. Perhaps it had flown away, after all. But her firm tread on the sea wall was full of eagerness, and sometimes unconsciously she found herself hurrying.

Frith saw the yellow light of Rhayader's lantern down by his little wharf, and she found him there. His sailboat was rocking gently on a flooding tide and he was loading supplies into her—water and food and bottles of brandy, gear and a spare sail. When he turned to the sound of her coming, she saw that he was pale, but that his dark eyes, usually so kind and placid, were glowing with excitement, and he was breathing heavily from his exertions.

Sudden alarm seized Frith. The snow goose was forgotten. "Philip! Ye be goin' away?"

Rhayader paused in his work to greet her, and there was something in his face, a glow and a look, that she had never seen there before.

"Frith! I am glad you came. Yes, I must go away. A little trip. I will come back." His usually kindly voice was hoarse with what was suppressed inside him.

Frith asked: "Where must ye go?"

Words came tumbling from Rhayader now. He must go to Dunkirk. A hundred miles across the North Sea. A British army was trapped there on the sands, awaiting destruction at the hands of the advancing Germans. The port was in flames, the position hopeless. He had heard it in the village when he had gone for supplies. Men were putting out from Chelmbury in answer to the government's call, every tug and fishing boat or power launch that could propel itself was heading across the sea to haul the men off the beaches to the transports and destroyers that could not reach the shallows, to rescue as many as possible from the Germans' fire.

Frith listened and felt her heart dying within her. He was saying that he would cross the sea in his little boat. It could take six men at a time; in a pinch, seven. He could make many trips from the beaches to the transports.

The girl was young, primitive, inarticulate. She did not understand war, or what had happened in France, or the meaning of the trapped army, but the blood within her told her that here was danger.

"Philip! Must 'ee go? You'll not come back. Why must it be 'ee?"

The fever seemed to have gone from Rhayader's soul with the first rush of words, and he explained it to her in terms that she could understand.

He said: "Men are huddled on the beaches like hunted birds, Frith, like the wounded and hunted birds we used to find and bring to sanctuary. Over them fly the steel peregrines, hawks and gyrfalcons, and they have no shelter from these iron birds of prey. They are lost and storm-driven and harried, like the *Princesse Perdue* you found and brought to me out of the marshes many years ago, and we healed her. They need help, my dear, as our wild creatures have needed help, and that is why I must go. It is something that I can do. Yes, I can. For once— for once I can be a man and play my part."

Frith stared at Rhayader. He had changed so. For the first time she saw that he was no longer ugly or misshapen or grotesque, but very beautiful. Things were turmoiling in her own soul, crying to be said, and she did not know how to say them.

"I'll come with 'ee, Philip."

Rhayader shook his head. "Your place in the boat would cause a soldier to be left behind, and another and another. I must go alone."

He donned rubber coat and boots and took to his boat. He waved and called back: "Good-by! Will you look after the birds until I return, Frith?"

Frith's hand come up, but only half, to wave too. "God speed you," she said, but gave it the Saxon turn. "I will take care of t' birds. Godspeed, Philip."

It was night now, bright with moon fragment and stars and northern glow. Frith stood on the sea wall and watched the sail gliding down the swollen estuary. Suddenly from the darkness behind her there came a rush of wings, and something swept past her into the air. In the light she saw the flash of white wings, black-tipped, and the thrust-forward head of the snow goose.

It rose and cruised over the lighthouse once and then headed down the winding creek where Rhayader's sail was slanting in the gaining breeze, and flew above him in slow, wide circles.

White sail and white bird were visible for a long time.

"Watch o'er him. Watch o'er him," Fritha whispered. When they were both out of sight at last, she turned and walked slowly, with bent head, back to the empty lighthouse.

Now the story becomes fragmentary, and one of these fragments is in the words of men on leave who told it in the public room of the Crown and Arrow, an East Chapel pub.

"A goose, a bloomin' goose, so 'elp me," said Private Potton, of His Majesty's London Rifles.

"Garn," said a bandy-legged artilleryman.

"A goose it was. Jock, 'ere, seed it same as me. It come flyin' down outa the muck an' stink an' smoke of Dunkirk that was over'ead. It was white, wiv black on its wings, an' it circles us like a bloomin' dive bomber. Jock, 'ere, 'e sez: 'We're done for. It's the hangel of death a-come for us.'

" 'Garn,' Hi sez, 'it's a ruddy goose, come over from 'ome wiv a message from Churchill, an' 'ow are we henjoying the bloomin' bathing. It's a omen, that's what it is, a bloody omen. We'll get out of this yet, me lad.'

"We was roostin' on the beach between Dunkirk an' Lapanny, like a lot o' bloomin' pigeons on Victoria Hembankment, waitin' for Jerry to pot us. 'E potted us good too. 'E was be'ind us an' flankin' us an' above us. 'E give us shrapnel and 'e give us H. E., an' 'e peppers us from the bloomin' hatmosphere with Jittersmiths.

"An' offshore is the *Kentish Maid,* a ruddy hexcursion scow wot Hi've taken many a trip on out of Margate in the summer, for two-and-six, waiting to take us off, 'arf a mile out from the bloomin' shallows.

"While we are lyin' there on the beach, done in an' cursin' becos there ain't no way to get out to the boat, a Stuka dives on 'er, an' 'is bombs drop alongside of 'er, throwin' up water like the bloomin' fountains in the palace gardens; a reg'lar display it was.

"Then a destroyer come up an' says: 'No, ye don't,' to the Stuka with ack-acks and pom-poms, but another Jerry dives on the destroyer, an' 'its 'er. Coo, did she go up! She burned before she sunk, an' the smoke an' the stink come driftin' inshore, all yellow an' black, an' out of it comes this bloomin' goose, a-circlin' around us trapped on the beach.

"An' then around a bend 'e comes in a bloody little sailboat, sailing along as cool as you please, like a bloomin' toff out for a pleasure spin on a Sunday hafternoon at 'Enley."

" 'Oo comes?" inquired a civilian.

" 'Im! 'Im that saved a lot of us. 'E sailed clean through a boil of machine-gun bullets from a Jerry in a Jittersmith wot was strafin'—a Ramsgate motorboat wot 'ad tried to take us off 'ad been sunk there 'arf an hour ago—the water was all frothin' with shell splashes an' bullets, but 'e didn't give it no mind, 'e didn't. 'E didn't 'ave no petrol to burn or hexplode, an' he sailed in between the shells.

"Into the shallows 'e come out of the black smoke of the burnin' destroyer, a little dark man wiv a beard, a bloomin' claw for a 'and, an' a 'ump on 'is back.

" 'E 'ad a rope in 'is teeth that was shinin' white out of 'is black beard, 'is good 'and on the tiller an' the crooked one beckonin' to us to come. An' over'ead, around and around, flies the ruddy goose.

"Jock, 'ere, says: 'Lawk, it's all over now. It's the bloody devil come for us 'imself. Hi must 'ave been struck an' don't know it.'

" 'Garn,' I sez, 'it's more like the good Lord, 'e looks to me, than any bloomin' devil.' 'E did, too, like the pictures from the Sunday-school books, wiv 'is white face and dark eyes an' beard an' all, and 'is bloomin' boat.

" 'Hi can take seven at a time,' 'e sings out when 'e's in close.

"Our horfficer shouts: 'Good, man! . . . You seven nearest, get in.'

"We waded out to where 'e was. Hi was that weary Hi couldn't clumb over the side, but 'e takes me by the collar of me tunic an' pulls, wiv a 'In ye go, lad. Come on. Next man.'

"An' in Hi went. Coo, 'e was strong, 'e was. Then 'e sets 'is sail, part of wot looks like a bloomin' sieve from machine-gun bullets, shouts: 'Keep down in the bottom of the boat, boys, in case we meet any of yer friends,' and we're off, 'im sittin' in the stern wiv 'is rope in 'is teeth, another in 'is crooked claw, an' 'is right 'and on the tiller, a-steerin' an' sailin' through the spray of the shells thrown by a land battery somewhere back of the coast. An' the bloomin' goose is flyin' around and around, 'onking above the wind and the row Jerry was makin', like a bloomin' Morris autermobile on Winchester bypass.

" 'Hi told you yon goose was a omen,' Hi sez to Jock. 'Look at 'im there, a bloomin' hangel of mercy.'

" 'Im at the tiller just looks up at the goose, wiv the

rope in 'is teeth, an' grins at 'er like 'e knows 'er a lifetime.

" 'E brung us out to the *Kentish Maid* and turns around and goes back for another load. 'E made trips all afternoon an' all night, too, because the bloody light of Dunkirk burning was bright enough to see by. Hi don't know 'ow many trips 'e made, but 'im an' a nobby Thames Yacht Club motorboat an' a big lifeboat from Poole that come along brought off all there was of us on that particular stretch of hell, without the loss of a man.

"We sailed when the last man was off, an' there was more than seven hunder' of us haboard a boat built to take two hunder'. 'E was still there when we left, an' 'e waved us good-by and sails off toward Dunkirk, and the bird wiv 'im. Blyme, it was queer to see that ruddy big goose flyin' around 'is boat, lit up by the fires like a white hangel against the smoke.

"A Stuka 'ad another go at us, 'arfway across, but 'e'd been stayin' up late nights, an' missed. By mornin' we was safe 'ome.

"Hi never did find out what become of 'im, or 'oo 'e was—'im wiv the 'ump an' 'is little sailboat. A bloody good man 'e was, that chap."

"Coo," said the artilleryman. "A ruddy big goose. Watcher know?"

In an officers' club on Brook Street, a retired naval officer, sixty-five years old, Commander Keith Brill-Oudener, was telling of his experiences during the evacuation of Dunkirk. Called out of bed at four o'clock in the morning, he had captained a lopsided Limehouse tug across the Strait of Dover, towing a string of Thames barges, which he brought back four times loaded with soldiers. On his last trip he came in with her funnel shot away and a hole in her side. But he got her back to Dover.

A naval-reserve officer, who had two Brixham trawlers and a Yarmouth drifter blasted out from under him in the last four days of the evacuation, said: "Did you run across that queer sort of legend about a wild goose? It was all up and down the beaches. You know how those things spring up. Some of the men I brought back were talking about it. It was supposed to have appeared at intervals the last days between Dunkirk and La Panne. If you saw it, you were eventually saved. That sort of thing."

"H'm'm'm," said Brill-Oudener, "a wild goose. I saw a tame one. Dashed strange experience. Tragic, in a way, too. And lucky for us. Tell you about it. Third trip back. Toward six o'clock we sighted a derelict small boat. Seemed to be a chap or a body in her. And a bird perched on the rail.

"We changed our course when we got nearer, and went over for a look-see. By Gad, it was a chap. Or had been, poor fellow. Machine-gunned, you know. Badly. Face down in the water. Bird was a goose, a tame one.

"We drifted close, but when one of our chaps reached over, the bird hissed at him and struck at him with her wings. Couldn't drive it off. Suddenly young Kettering, who was with me, gave a hail and pointed to starboard. Big mine floating by. One of Jerry's beauties. If we'd kept on our course we'd have piled right into it. Ugh! Head on. We let it get a hundred yards astern of the last barge, and the men blew it up with rifle-fire.

"When we turned our attention to the derelict again, she was gone. Sunk. Concussion, you know. Chap with her. He must have been lashed to her. The bird had got up and was circling. Three times, like a plane saluting. Dashed queer feeling. Then she flew off to the west.

Lucky thing for us we went over to have a look, eh? Odd that you should mention a goose."

Fritha remained alone at the little lighthouse on the Great Marsh, taking care of the pinioned birds, waiting for she knew not what. The first days she haunted the sea wall, watching; though she knew it was useless. Later she roamed through the storerooms of the lighthouse building with their stacks of canvases on which Rhayader had captured every mood and light of the desolate country and the wondrous, graceful, feathered things that inhabited it.

Among them she found the picture that Rhayader had painted of her from memory so many years ago, when she was still a child, and had stood, wind-blown and timid, at his threshold, hugging an injured bird to her.

The picture and the things she saw in it stirred her as nothing ever had before, for much of Rhayader's soul had gone into it. Strangely, it was the only time he had painted the snow goose, the lost wild creature, storm-driven from another land, that to each had brought a friend, and which, in the end, returned to her with the message that she would never see him again.

Long before the snow goose had come dropping out of a crimsoned eastern sky to circle the lighthouse in a last farewell. Fritha, from the ancient powers of the blood that was in her, knew that Rhayader would not return.

And so, when one sunset she heard the high-pitched, well-remembered note cried from the heavens, it brought no instant of false hope to her heart. This moment, it seemed, she had lived before many times.

She came running to the sea wall and turned her eyes, not toward the distant sea whence a sail might come, but to the sky from whose flaming arches plummeted the snow goose. Then the sight, the sound, and the solitude surrounding broke the dam within her and released the surging, overwhelming truth of her love, let it well forth in tears.

Wild spirit called to wild spirit, and she seemed to be flying with the great bird, soaring with it in the evening sky, and hearkening to Rhayader's message.

Sky and earth were trembling with it and filled her beyond the bearing of it. "Frith! Fritha! Frith, my love. Good-by, my love." The white pinions, black-tipped, were beating it out upon her heart, and her heart was answering: "Philip, I love 'ee."

For a moment Frith thought the snow goose was going to land in the old enclosure, as the pinioned geese set up a welcoming gabble. But it only skimmed low, then soared up again, flew in a wide, graceful spiral once around the old light, and then began to climb.

Watching it, Frith saw no longer the snow goose but the soul of Rhayader taking farewell of her before departing forever.

She was no longer flying with it, but earthbound. She stretched her arms up into the sky and stood on tiptoes, reaching, and cried: "Godspeed! Godspeed, Philip!"

Frith's tears were stilled. She stood watching silently long after the goose had vanished. Then she went into the lighthouse and secured the picture that Rhayader had painted of her. Hugging it to her breast, she wended her way homeward along the old sea wall.

Each night, for many weeks thereafter, Frith came to the lighthouse and fed the pinioned birds. Then one early morning a German pilot on a dawn raid mistook the old abandoned light for an active military objective, dived onto it, a screaming steel hawk, and blew it and all it contained into oblivion.

That evening when Fritha came, the sea had moved in

through the breached walls and covered it over. Nothing was left to break the utter desolation. No marsh fowl had dared to return. Only the frightless gulls wheeled and soared and mewed their plaint over the place where it had been.

The Small Miracle

To St. Francis
a man among saints

The beautiful setting of Assisi is clearly essential for the purposes of this story. But the characters exist only in the imagination of the author and are not based upon any real persons. They are delineated as they are purely literary reasons

APPROACHING Assisi via the chalky, dusty road that twists its way up Monte Subasio, now revealing, now concealing the exquisite little town, as it winds its way through olive and cypress groves, you eventually reach a division where your choice lies between an upper and a lower route.

If you select the latter, you soon find yourself entering Assisi through the twelfth-century archway of the denticulated door of St. Francis. But if, seduced by the clear air, the wish to mount even closer to the canopy of blue Italian sky and expose still more of the delectable view of the rich Umbrian valley below, you choose the upper way, you and your vehicle eventually become inextricably entangled in the welter of humanity, oxen, goats, bawling calves, mules, fowl, children, pigs, booths and carts gathered at the market place outside the walls.

It is here you would be most likely to encounter Pepino, with his donkey Violetta, hard at work, turning his hand to anything whereby a small boy and a strong, willing beast of burden could win for themselves the crumpled ten and twenty lira notes needed to buy food and pay for lodging in the barn of Niccolo the stableman.

Pepino and Violetta were everything to each other.

They were a familiar sight about Assisi and its immediate environs—the thin brown boy, ragged and barefooted, with the enormous dark eyes, large ears, and close-cropped, upstanding hair, and the dust-colored little donkey with the Mona Lisa smile.

Pepino was ten years old and an orphan, his father, mother and near relatives having been killed in the war. In self-reliance, wisdom and demeanor he was, of course, much older, a circumstance aided by his independence, for Pepino was an unusual orphan in that having a heritage he need rely on no one. Pepino's heritage was Violetta.

She was a good, useful and docile donkey, alike as any other with friendly, gentle eyes, soft taupe-colored muzzle, and long, pointed brown ears, with one exception that distinguished her. Violetta had a curious expression about the corners of her mouth, as though she was smiling gently over something that amused or pleased her. Thus, no matter what kind of work, or how much she was asked to do, she always appeared to be performing it with a smile of quiet satisfaction. The combination of Pepino's dark lustrous eyes and Violetta's smile was so harmonious that people favored them and they were able not only to earn enough for their keep but, aided and advised by Father Damico, the priest of their parish, to save a little as well.

There were all kinds of things they could do—carry loads of wood or water, deliver purchases carried in the panniers that thumped against Violetta's sides, hire out to help pull a cart mired in the mud, aid in the olive harvest, and even, occasionally, help some citizen who was too encumbered with wine to reach his home on foot, by means of a four-footed taxi with Pepino walking beside to see that the drunkard did not fall off.

But this was not the only reason for the love that

51

existed between boy and donkey, for Violetta was more than just the means of his livelihood. She was mother to him, and father, brother, playmate, companion, and comfort. At night, in the straw of Niccolo's stable, Pepino slept curled up close to her when it was cold, his head pillowed on her neck.

Since the mountainside was a rough world for a small boy, he was sometimes beaten or injured, and then he could creep to her for comfort and Violetta would gently nuzzle his bruises. When there was joy in his heart, he shouted songs into her waving ears; when he was lonely and hurt, he could lean his head against her soft, warm flank and cry out his tears.

On his part, he fed her, watered her, searched her for ticks and parasites, picked stones from her hoofs,

scratched and groomed and curried her, lavished affection on her, particularly when they were alone, while in public he never beat her with the donkey stick more than was necessary. For this treatment Violetta made a god of Pepino, and repaid him with loyalty, obedience and affection.

Thus, when one day in the early spring Violetta fell ill, it was the most serious thing that had ever happened to Pepino. It began first with an unusual lethargy that would respond neither to stick nor caresses, nor the young, strident voice urging her on. Later Pepino observed other symptoms and visible loss of weight. Her ribs, once so well padded, began to show through her sides. But most distressing, either through a change in the conformation of her head, due to growing thinner, or because of the distress of the illness, Violetta lost her enchanting and lovable smile.

Drawing upon his carefully hoarded reserves of lira notes and parting with several of the impressive denomination of a hundred, Pepino called in Dr. Bartoli, the vet.

The vet examined her in good faith, dosed her, and tried his best; but she did not improve and, instead, continued to lose weight and grow weaker. He hummed and hawed then and said, "Well, now, it is hard to say. It might be one thing, such as the bite of a fly new to this district, or another, such as a germ settling in the intestine." Either way, how could one tell? There had been a similar case in Foligno and another in a far-away town. He recommended resting the beast and feeding her lightly. If the illness passed from her and God willed, she might live. Otherwise, she would surely die and there would be an end to her suffering.

After he had gone away, Pepino put his cropped head on Violetta's heaving flank and wept unrestrainedly. But then, when the storm, induced by the fear of losing his only companion in the world, had subsided, he knew what he must do. If there was no help for Violetta on earth, the appeal must be registered above. His plan was nothing less than to take Violetta into the crypt beneath the lower church of the Basilica of St. Francis, where rested the remains of the Saint who had so dearly loved God's creations, including all the feathered and the four-footed brothers and sisters who served Him. There he would beg St. Francis to heal her. Pepino had no doubt that the Saint would do so when he saw Violetta.

These things Pepino knew from Father Damico, who had a way of talking about St. Francis as though he were a living person who might still be encountered in his frayed cowl, bound with a hemp cord at the middle, merely by turning a corner of the Main Square in Assisi or by walking down one of the narrow, cobbled streets.

And besides, there was a precedent. Giani, his friend, the son of Niccolo the stableman, had taken his sick kitten into the crypt and asked St. Francis to heal her, and the cat had got well—at least half well, anyway, for her hind legs still dragged a little; but at least she had not died. Pepino felt that if Violetta were to die, it would be the end of everything for him.

Thereupon, with considerable difficulty, he persuaded the sick and shaky donkey to rise, and with urgings and caresses and minimum use of the stick drove her through the crooked streets of Assisi and up the hill to the Basilica of St. Francis. At the beautiful twin portal of the lower church he respectfully asked Fra Bernard, who was on duty there, for permission to take Violetta down to St. Francis, so that she might be made well again.

Fra Bernard was a new monk, and, calling Pepino a young and impious scoundrel, ordered him and his donkey to be off. It was strictly forbidden to bring livestock into the church, and even to think of taking an ass into the crypt of St. Francis was a desecration. And besides, how did he imagine she would get down there when the narrow, winding staircase was barely wide enough to accommodate humans in single file, much less four-footed animals? Pepino must be a fool as well as a shiftless rascal.

As ordered, Pepino retreated from the portal, his arm about Violetta's neck, and bethought himself of what he must do next to succeed in his purpose, for while he was disappointed at the rebuff he had received, he was not at all discouraged.

Despite the tragedy that had struck Pepino's early life and robbed him of his family, he really considered himself a most fortunate boy, compared with many, since he had acquired not only a heritage to aid him in earning a living but also an important precept by which to live.

This maxim, the golden key to success, had been left with Pepino, together with bars of chocolate, chewing gum, peanut brittle, soap, and other delights, by a corporal in the United States Army who had, in the six months he had been stationed in the vicinity of Assisi, been Pepino's demigod and hero. His name was Francis Xavier O'Halloran, and what he told Pepino before he departed out of his life forever was, "If you want to get ahead in this world, kid, don't never take no for an answer. Get it?" Pepino never forgot this important advice.

He thought now that his next step was clear; nevertheless, he went first to his friend and adviser, Father Damico, for confirmation.

Father Damico, who had a broad head, lustrous eyes, and shoulders shaped as though they had been especially designed to support the burdens laid upon them by his parishioners, said, "You are within your rights, my son, in taking your request to the lay Supervisor and it lies within his power to grant or refuse it."

There was no malice in the encouragement he thus gave Pepino, but it was also true that he was not loath to see the Supervisor brought face to face with an example of pure and innocent faith. For in his private opinion that worthy man was too much concerned with the twin churches that formed the Basilica and the crypt as a tourist attraction. He, Father Damico, could not see why the child should not have his wish, but, of course, it was out of his jurisdiction. He was, however, curious about how the Supervisor would react, even though he thought he knew in advance.

However, he did not impart his fears to Pepino and merely called after him as he was leaving, "And if the little one cannot be got in from above, there is another entrance from below, through the old church, only it has been walled up for a hundred years. But it could be opened. You might remind the Supervisor when you see him. He knows where it is."

Pepino thanked him and went back alone to the Basilica and the monastery attached to it and asked permission to see the Supervisor.

This personage was an accessible man, and even though he was engaged in a conversation with the Bishop, he sent for Pepino, who walked into the cloister gardens where he waited respectfully for the two great men to finish.

The two dignitaries were walking up and down, and Pepino wished it were the Bishop who was to say yea or nay to his request, as he looked the kindlier of the two, the Supervisor appearing to have more the expression of a merchant. The boy pricked up his ears, because, as it happened, they were speaking of St. Francis, and the

Bishop was just remarking with a sigh, "He has been gone too long from this earth. The lesson of his life is plain to all who can read. But who in these times will pause to do so?"

The Supervisor said, "His tomb in the crypt attracts many to Assisi. But in a Holy Year, relics are even better. If we but had the tongue of the Saint, or a lock of his hair, or a fingernail."

The Bishop had a far-away look in his eyes, and he was shaking his head gently. "It is a message we are in need of, my dear Supervisor, a message from a great heart that would speak to us across the gap of seven centuries to remind us of The Way." And here he paused and coughed, for he was a polite man and noticed that Pepino was waiting.

The Supervisor turned also and said, "Ah yes, my son, what is it that I can do for you?"

Pepino said, "Please, sir, my donkey Violetta is very sick. The Doctor Bartoli has said he can do nothing more and perhaps she will die. Please, I would like permission to take her into the tomb of Saint Francis and ask him to cure her. He loved all animals, and particularly little donkeys. I am sure he will make her well."

The Supervisor looked shocked. "A donkey. In the crypt. However did you come to that idea?"

Pepino explained about Giani and his sick kitten, while the Bishop turned away to hide a smile.

But the Supervisor was not smiling. He asked, "How did this Giani succeed in smuggling a kitten into the tomb?"

Since it was all over, Pepino saw no reason for not telling, and replied, "Under his coat, sir."

The Supervisor made a mental note to warn the brothers to keep a sharper eye out for small boys or other persons with suspicious-looking lumps under their outer clothing.

"Of course we can have no such goings on," he said. "The next thing you know, everyone would be coming, bringing a sick dog, or an ox, or a goat, or even a pig. And then where should we end up? A veritable sty."

"But, sir," Pepino pleaded, "no one need know. We would come and go so very quickly."

The Supervisor's mind played. There was something touching about the boy—the bullet head, the enormous eyes, the jug-handle ears. And yet, what if he permitted it and the donkey then died, as seemed most likely if Dr. Bartoli had said there was no further hope? Word was sure to get about, and the shrine would suffer from it. He wondered what the Bishop was thinking and how *he* would solve the problem.

He equivocated: "And besides, even if we were to allow it, you would never be able to get your donkey around the turn at the bottom of the stairs. So, you see, it is quite impossible."

"But there is another entrance," Pepino said. "From the old church. It has not been used for a long time, but it could be opened just this once—couldn't it?"

The Supervisor was indignant. "What are you saying—destroy church property? The entrance has been walled up for over a century, ever since the new crypt was built."

The Bishop thought he saw a way out and said gently to the boy, "Why do you not go home and pray to Saint Francis to assist you? If you open your heart to him and have faith, he will surely hear you."

"But it wouldn't be the same," Pepino cried, and his voice was shaking with the sobs that wanted to come. "I must take her where Saint Francis can see her. She isn't like any other old donkey—Violetta has the sweetest smile. She does not smile any more since she has been so ill. But perhaps she would, just once more for Saint Francis. And when he saw it he would not be able to resist her, and he would make her well. I know he would!"

The Supervisor knew his ground now. He said, "I am sorry, my son, but the answer is no."

But even through his despair and the bitter tears he shed as he went away, Pepino knew that if Violetta was to live he must not take no for an answer.

"Who is there, then?" Pepino asked of Father Damico later. "Who is above the Supervisor and my lord the Bishop who might tell them to let me take Violetta into the crypt?"

Father Damico's stomach felt cold as he thought of the dizzying hierarchy between Assisi and Rome. Nevertheless, he explained as best he could, concluding with, "And at the top is His Holiness, the Pope himself. Surely his heart would be touched by what has happened if you were able to tell him, for he is a great and good man. But he is busy with important weighty affairs, Pepino, and it would be impossible for him to see you."

Pepino went back to Niccolo's stable, where he ministered to Violetta, fed and watered her and rubbed her muzzle a hundred times. Then he withdrew his money from the stone jar buried under the straw and counted it. He had almost three hundred lire. A hundred of it he set aside and promised to his friend Giani if he would look after Violetta, while Pepino was gone, as if she were his own. Then he patted her once more, brushed away the tears that had started again at the sight of how thin she was, put on his jacket, and went out on the high road, where, using his thumb as he had learned from Corporal Francis Xavier O'Halloran, he got a lift in a lorry going to Foligno and the main road. He was on his way to Rome to see the Holy Father.

Never had any small boy looked quite so infinitesimal and forlorn as Pepino standing in the boundless and almost deserted, since it was early in the morning, St. Peter's Square. Everything towered over him—the massive dome of St. Peter's, the obelisk of Caligula, the Bernini colonnades. Everything contrived to make him look pinched and miserable in his bare feet, torn trousers, and ragged jacket. Never was a boy more overpowered, lonely, and frightened, or carried a greater burden of unhappiness in his heart.

For now that he was at last in Rome, the gigantic proportions of the buildings and monuments, their awe and majesty, began to sap his courage, and he seemed to have a glimpse into the utter futility and hopelessness of

60

his mission. And then there would arise in his mind a picture of the sad little donkey who did not smile any more, her heaving flanks and clouded eyes, and who would surely die unless he could find help for her. It was thoughts like these that enabled him finally to cross the piazza and timidly approach one of the smaller side entrances to the Vatican.

The Swiss guard, in his slashed red, yellow, and blue uniform, with his long halberd, looked enormous and forbidding. Nevertheless, Pepino edged up to him and said, "Please, will you take me to see the Pope? I wish to speak to him about my donkey Violetta, who is very ill and may die unless the Pope will help me."

The guard smiled, not unkindly, for he was used to these ignorant and innocent requests, and the fact that it came from a dirty, ragged little boy, with eyes like ink pools and a round head from which the ears stood out like the handles on a cream jug, made it all the more harmless. But, nevertheless, he was shaking his head as he smiled, and then said that His Holiness was a very busy man and could not be seen. And the guard grounded his halberd with a thud and let it fall slantwise across the door to show that he meant business.

Pepino backed away. What good was his precept in the face of such power and majesty? And yet the memory of what Corporal O'Halloran had said told him that he must return to the Vatican yet once again.

At the side of the piazza he saw an old woman sitting under an umbrella, selling little bouquets and nosegays of spring flowers—daffodils and jonquils, snowdrops and white narcissus, Parma violets and lilies of the valley, vari-colored carnations, pansies, and tiny sweetheart roses. Some of the people visiting St. Peter's liked to place these on the altar of their favorite saint. The flowers were crisp and fresh from the market, and many of

them had glistening drops of water still clinging to their petals.

Looking at them made Pepino think of home and Father Damico and what he had said of the love St. Francis had for flowers. Father Damico had the gift of making everything he thought and said sound like poetry. And Pepino came to the conclusion that if St. Francis, who had been a holy man, had been so fond of flowers, perhaps the Pope, who according to his position was even holier, would love them, too.

For fifty lire he bought a tiny bouquet in which a spray of lilies of the valley rose from a bed of dark violets and small red roses crowded next to yellow pansies all tied about with leaf and feather fern and paper lace.

From a stall where postcards and souvenirs were sold, he begged pencil and paper, and laboriously composed a note:

Dear and most sacred Holy Father: These flowers are for you. Please let me see you and tell you about my donkey Violetta who is dying, and they will not let me take her to see Saint Francis so that he may cure her. I live in the town of Assisi, but I have come all the way here to see you
Your loving Pepino.

Thereupon, he returned to the door, placed the bouquet and the note in the hand of the Swiss guard, and begged, "Please take these up to the Pope. I am sure he will see me when he receives the flowers and reads what I have written."

The guard had not expected this. The child and the flowers had suddenly placed him in a dilemma from which he could not extricate himself in the presence of those large and trusting eyes. However, he was not without experience in handling such matters. He had only to place a colleague at his post, go to the Guard Room, throw the flowers and the note into the wastepaper basket, absent himself for a sufficient length of time, and then return to tell the boy that His Holiness thanked him for the gift of the flowers and regretted that press of important business made it impossible for him to grant him an audience.

This little subterfuge the guard put into motion at once; but when he came to completing the next-to-last act in it, he found to his amazement that somehow he could not bring himself to do it. There was the wastepaper basket, yawning to receive the offering, but

the little nosegay seemed to be glued to his fingers. How gay, sweet, and cool the flowers were. What thoughts they brought to his mind of spring in the green valleys of his far-off canton of Luzern. He saw again the snow-capped mountains of his youth, the little gingerbread houses, the gray, soft-eyed cattle grazing in the blossom-carpeted meadows, and he heard the heart-warming tinkling of their bells.

Dazed by what had happened to him, he left the Guard Room and wandered through the corridors, for he did not know where to go or what to do with his burden. He was eventually encountered by a busy little Monsignor, one of the vast army of clerks and secretaries employed in the Vatican, who paused, astonished at the sight of the burly guard helplessly contemplating a tiny posy.

And thus occurred the minor miracle whereby Pepino's plea and offering crossed the boundary in the palace that divided the mundane from the spiritual, the lay from the ecclesiastical.

For to the great relief of the guard, the Monsignor took over the burning articles that he had been unable to relinquish; and this priest they touched, too, as it is the peculiar power of flowers that while they are universal and spread their species over the world, they invoke in each beholder the dearest and most cherished memories.

In this manner, the little bouquet passed on and upward from a hand to hand, pausing briefly in the possession of the clerk of the Apostolic Chamber, the Privy Almoner, the Papal Sacristan, the Master of the Sacred Palaces, the Papal Chamberlain. The dew vanished from the flowers; they began to lose their freshness and to wilt, passing from hand to hand. And yet they retained their magic, the message of love and memories that rendered it impossible for any of these intermediaries to dispose of them.

Eventually, then, they were deposited with the missive that accompanied them on the desk of the man for whom they had been destined. He read the note and then sat there silently contemplating the blossoms. He closed his eyes for a moment, the better to entertain the picture that arose in his mind of himself as a small Roman boy taken on a Sunday into the Alban Hills, where for the first time he saw violets growing wild.

When he opened his eyes at last, he said to his secretary, "Let the child be brought here. I will see him."

Thus it was that Pepino at last came into the presence of the Pope, seated at his desk in his office. Perched on the edge of a chair next to him, Pepino told the whole story about Violetta, his need to take her into the tomb of St. Francis, about the Supervisor who was preventing him, and all about Father Damico, too, and the second entrance to the crypt, Violetta's smile, and his love for her—everything, in fact, that was in his heart and that now poured forth to the sympathetic man sitting quietly behind the desk.

And when, at the end of half an hour, he was ushered from the presence, he was quite sure he was the happiest boy in the world. For he had not only the blessing of the Pope, but also, under his jacket, two letters, one addressed to the lay Supervisor of the Monastery of Assisi and the other to Father Damico. No longer did he feel small and overwhelmed when he stepped out on to the square again past the astonished but delighted Swiss guard. He felt as though he could give one leap and a bound and fly back to his Violetta's side.

Nevertheless, he had to give heed to the more practical side of transportation. He inquired his way to a bus that took him to where the Via Flaminia became a country road stretching to the north, then plied his thumb backed by his eloquent eyes, and before nightfall of that day, with good luck, was home in Assisi.

After a visit to Violetta had assured him that she had been well looked after and at least was no worse than she had been before his departure, Pepino proudly went to Father Damico and presented his letters as he had been instructed to do.

The Father fingered the envelope for the Supervisor and then, with a great surge of warmth and happiness, read the one addressed to himself. He said to Pepino, "Tomorrow we will take the Supervisor's letter to him. He will summon masons and the old door will be broken down and you will be able to take Violetta into the tomb

and pray there for her recovery. The Pope himself has approved it."

The Pope, of course, had not written the letters personally. They had been composed with considerable delight and satisfaction by the Cardinal-Secretary, backed by Papal authority, who said in his missive to Father Damico:

> *Surely the Supervisor must know that in his lifetime the blessed Saint Francis was accompanied to chapel by a little lamb that used to follow him about Assisi. Is an* asinus *any less created by God because his coat is rougher and his ears longer?*

69

And he wrote also of another matter, which Father Damico imparted to Pepino in his own way.

He said, "Pepino, there is something you must understand before we go to see the Abbot. It is your hope that because of your faith in St. Francis he will help you and heal your donkey. But had you thought, perhaps, that he who dearly cared for all of God's creatures might come to love Violetta so greatly that he would wish to have her at his side in Eternity?"

A cold terror gripped Pepino as he listened. He managed to say, "No, Father, I had not thought—" The priest continued: "Will you go to the crypt only to ask, Pepino, or will you also, if necessary, be prepared to give?"

Everything in Pepino cried out against the possibility of losing Violetta, even to someone as beloved as St. Francis. Yet when he raised his stricken face and looked into the lustrous eyes of Father Damico, there was something in their depths that gave him the courage to whisper, "I will give—if I must. But, oh, I hope he will let her stay with me just a little longer."

The clink of the stonemason's pick rang again and again through the vaulted chamber of the lower church, where the walled-up door of the passageway leading to the crypt was being removed. Nearby waited the Supervisor and his friend the Bishop, Father Damico, and Pepino, large-eyed, pale, and silent. The boy kept his arms about the neck of Violetta and his face pressed to hers. The little donkey was very shaky on her legs and could barely stand.

The Supervisor watched humbly and impassively while broken bricks and clods of mortar fell as the breach widened and the freed current of air from the passage swirled the plaster dust in clouds. He was a just man for all his weakness and had invited the Bishop to witness his rebuke.

A portion of the wall proved obstinate. The mason attacked the archway at the side to weaken its support. Then the loosened masonry began to tumble again. A narrow passageway was effected, and through the opening they could see the distant flicker of the candles placed at the altar wherein rested the remains of St. Francis.

Pepino stirred towards the opening. Or was it Violetta who had moved nervously, frightened by the unaccustomed place and noises? Father Damico said, "Wait," and Pepino held her; but the donkey's uncertain feet slipped on the rubble and then lashed out in panic, striking the side of the archway where it had been weakened. A brick fell out. A crack appeared.

Father Damico leaped and pulled boy and animal out of the way as, with a roar, the side of the arch collapsed, laying bare a piece of the old wall and the hollow behind it before everything vanished in a cloud of dust.

But when the dust settled, the Bishop, his eyes starting from his head, was pointing to something that rested in a niche of the hollow just revealed. It was a small, gray, leaden box. Even from there they could see the year 1226, when St. Francis died, engraved on the side, and the large initial "F."

The Bishop's breath came out like a sigh. "Ah, could it be? The legacy of Saint Francis! Fra Leo mentions it. It was hidden away centuries ago, and no one had ever been able to find it since."

The Supervisor said hoarsely, "The contents! Let us see what is inside—it may be valuable!"

The Bishop hesitated. "Perhaps we had best wait. For this is in itself a miracle, this finding."

But Father Damico, who was a poet and to whom St. Francis was a living spirit, cried, "Open it, I beg of you! All who are here are humble. Surely Heaven's plan has guided us to it."

The Abbot held the lantern. The mason with his careful, honest workman's hands deftly loosed the bindings and pried the lid of the airtight box. It opened with an ancient creaking of its hinge and revealed what had been placed there more than seven centuries before.

There was a piece of hempen cord, knotted as though, perhaps, once it had been worn about the waist. Caught in the knot, as fresh as though it had grown but yesterday, was a single sprig of wheat. Dried and preserved, there lay, too, the stem and starry flower of a mountain primrose and, next to it, one downy feather from a tiny meadow bird.

Silently the men stared at these objects from the past to try to read their meaning, and Father Damico wept, for to him they brought the vivid figure of the Saint, half-blinded, worn and fragile, the cord knotted at his waist, singing, striding through a field of wheat. The flower might have been the first discovered by him after a winter's snow, and addressed as "Sister Cowslip," and praised for her tenderness and beauty. As though he were transported there, Father Damico saw the little field bird fly trustingly to Francis' shoulder and chirrup and nestle there and leave a feather in his hand. His heart was so full he thought he could not bear it.

The Bishop, too, was close to tears as, in his own way, he interpreted what they had found. "Ah, what could be clearer than the message of the Saint? Poverty, love, and faith. This is his bequest to all of us."

Pepino said, "Please, lords and sirs, may Violetta and I go into the crypt now?"

They had forgotten him. Now they started up from their contemplation of the touching relics.

Father Damico cleared the tears from his eyes. The doorway was freed now, and there was room for boy and donkey to pass. "Ah, yes," he said. "Yes, Pepino. You may enter now. And may God go with you."

The hoofs of the donkey went sharply *clip-clop, clip-clop* on the ancient flagging of the passageway. Pepino did not support her now, but walked beside, hand just resting lightly and lovingly on her neck. His round, cropped head with the outstanding ears was held high, and his shoulders were bravely squared.

And to Father Damico it seemed, as they passed, whether because of the uneven light and the dancing shadows, or because he wished it so, that the ghost, the merest wisp, the barest suspicion of a smile had returned to the mouth of Violetta.

Thus the watchers saw boy and donkey silhouetted against the flickering oil lamps and altar candles of the crypt as they went forward to complete their pilgrimage of faith.

Ludmila

To Baroness Ludmila Von Falz-Fein

PART way up the valley from Steg, in the Principality of Liechtenstein, where the torrent Malbun comes tumbling down its glacial bed from the peaks of the *Ochsenkopf* and *Silberhorn,* you will find the shrine of Saint Ludmila, *die heilige Notburga,* in a niche cut into the solid rock above the rushing waters.

It is a sweet figure in milkmaid's dress with the golden rays of the sun behind her head in place of the usual halo. In one hand she holds a harvesting sickle, and in the other a milk jug, for she is the patron saint of the dairymen, the herdsmen, milkers, butter separators and cheese makers, and the taupe-colored Alpine cattle with the broad heads, curving horns and large, gentle eyes are under her special protection.

Indeed, her connection with such is plain for all to see since beneath the feet of the figure there is affixed the whitened skull and grayish horns of what must once have been rather a small cow.

The younger generations, no longer brought up as were their fathers on the legends of the mountains, are unaware of its significance, but many of the local patriarchs remember what they learned at their mother's knee of the miracle that happened more than a hundred years ago, performed by the holy Notburga, the sainted milkmaid, the time of the annual return of the cattle at the end of the summer from the high pasturage to Baduz in the Rhine Valley below.

All those connected with the event are long since dead, Alois, the bearded, hardheaded, chief herdsman and his brown-haired daughter, Ludmila, who was then only seven, and named after the saint, Father Polda, the mountain priest, chaplain of Steg, and of course the little Weakling, whose skull and horns adorn the shrine of the patron saint of all milch cows.

However, you may still see the gay and colorful ceremony that takes place in Liechtenstein each autumn when the first threat of snow comes to the high passes and the cattle begin to cough in the early gusts of cold wind that sweep down from the *Sareiserjoch* and the glaciers behind the *Wildberg* and *Panülerkopf*.

There is a valley tucked away behind the granite wall of the Three Sisters above Schaan, in Liechtenstein, the *Saminatal,* leading to Malbun, five thousand feet above the meandering Rhine. It is famous for its rich grass and quiet, protected pasturage, where are to be encountered from time to time scattered plants of that herb not found in the lowlands, one of the rare *Garbengewächse,* of the Species *Alchemilla,* which the Liechtensteiners call by the beautiful name of *Mutterkraut*—or "Mothers weed," for it is believed to increase the flow of milk, and the herdsmen are invariably on the lookout for the yellow-flowered broad-leafed plants which seem to grow best in those shaded spots where the snow has lain the longest during the winter when the valley is buried under snow and ice.

It is the custom of the peasants in Liechtenstein each spring to send their cattle up into the mountains and through the tunnel cut through a quarter mile of solid rock near Steg that gives access to this hidden, enchanted valley. They go in charge of herdsmen, dairymen, and cheese makers, who move up with the beasts, taking their families with them in horse-drawn wooden carts.

There they remain for the entire summer, living in the high Alpine huts, tending the cattle at pasturage, milking them, making the rich yellow cheeses and creamy butter on the spot and keeping careful record of the yield of each animal. There is no contact with the valley below. Herds and herdsmen vanish, not to reappear until mid-September.

But then, what a day!

The peasants come from miles around to gather at Gnalp, below the Kulm at the mouth of the tunnel. From Triesen, Vaduz, Balzers, and Schaan, in the *Rheintal* below, the citizens climb the mountain, lining the winding roads, to cheer and wave to the returning wanderers, crowding as close as possible to see which and whose cow will be the first to emerge from the tunnel, leading all the rest as signal of her championship.

The *Abfahrt* or descent takes place in the early

morning with the sun shining over the *Rheintal,* warming the first nip in the clear mountain air. At first there is only the eager chatter of the citizens as they wait, the cries of children at play, and the distant rush of mountain torrents. But then as a deep, hollow booming is heard from the dark recesses of the tunnel, an expectant hush falls upon the waiting throng. It is the sound of the giant bell of black metal, cast especially for this occasion, and hung around the neck of the leading animal.

Louder and louder grows the clanging, as the herd approaches, stiller and stiller the people until with all the drama of a star actor suddenly bursting upon the stage, the champion of champions emerges into the light and stands for a moment, framed by the dark mouth of the tunnel.

She presents a strange and beautiful sight. Around her soft, fawn-colored neck suspended from a shining dark leather collar hangs the huge copper bell decorated on all sides with silver hearts and stars and fitted with a silver clapper. This with her position as leader of the procession confirms her as best cow of the high pastures, best cow of the summer, best beast in the land.

On her forehead she wears a crimson heart or cross to indicate her milk or cream has passed the average. But most striking of all, revealing her as first in her herd in yield of milk, butter, and cheese, her one-legged milking stool has been affixed to the broad and noble head between the graceful sweep of the horns.

It is tied there upside down like the gay hat of a maid in spring, beribboned with streamers of the red and blue of Liechtenstein, crimson and white, silver and gold. A wreath fashioned of laurel leaves is woven about her head; cockades of red, white, and blue are at her ears, bunches of meadow flowers make gay the leather of her collar.

82

One can only gaze at her with astonishment and admiration, for her simple, unobtrusive, natural beauty has been enhanced a hundredfold.

The procession winds out of the long tunnel and down the mountainside, the champions, the next best, the winners in minor classes, each with heart or cross, or milking stool bound upside down between her horns, then the horses garlanded and bedecked, drawing the family carts, the herdsmen and dairymen wearing rosettes of colored ribbon on their shirts and crimson and azure cockades in their hats, bearing signs "All of us are returning." The signs too are cheered. No accidents, no illnesses, no deaths. God had been good. Saint Rocchus and Saint Ludmila, the holy Notburga, have watched over them and kept them from harm. Another year has passed. In the flower-garlanded carts the fat tubs of butter and the cheeses piled high like red and yellow cannon balls denote prosperity and the wealth that the Creator, through nature, has seen fit to bestow upon His children.

And last of all, seemingly shamefaced, sad-eyed as though they knew that they had failed, without insignia, or touch of color at horns or flank, unattended except for the work dogs yapping at their heels and the herdsman's apprentice bringing up the rear, come those animals of more common breed or less energy, who have failed to distinguish themselves in the production of milk, or the percentage of butter fat in their cream, or good solid proteins in the cannon-ball cheeses. From their unhappy expressions you would almost swear they knew they were inferior.

By the time they emerge from the tunnel there is no one left to greet them, or even notice them; the crowds have gone off down the mountain, accompanying the colorful cavalcade of the successful beasts, leaving the others to bring up the rear as best they may.

It is a day of excitement, rejoicing, and felicitation, with the owners of the winners crowding the cafés and opening bottles of red Vaduzer wine to the herdsmen and dairymen. It is a great occasion for the winners.

No longer in the general rejoicing and carousing incident to this harvest ceremony is much thought directed toward the holy Notburga, that fourteenth-century milkmaid and simple serving girl who because of her piety, faith, and devotion to the Virgin Mary, became a saint under her given name of Ludmila, devoted to the care of Alpine cattle and their herdsmen.

The skiers returning in the winter at dusk from the slopes of Malbun throw her hardly a glance, and the Ave that once used to be sung to her nightly by the herdsmen is now locked between the covers of a book instead of in the hearts of the people.

It was different in the old days, before belief in miracles, magic, and all the magical creatures that once inhabited the glens, ravines, and dark forests went from the mountains. Nature spoke more vividly to the people than it does today.

In those times there were still witches, elves, kobolds, and little hairy wild men, good and evil fairies and saints that took on human guise and came down from Heaven to assist the pious or punish the wicked. Werewolves roamed the slopes and the scaly dragon with poisonous breath and deadly sting inhabited the rocky caverns. Even the great eagles perched on lofty crags, peering down in search of the whistling marmots, were regarded with superstition.

It was just at the end of this period and the beginning of modern times, so say the old men who remember this bit as told by their mothers, or that version handed down in an old mountain song, along with some yellowed sheets of notes left by Father Polda in the tiny chapel at Steg, that the strange affair of the little weakling cow who was deemed good for nothing took place.

Perhaps it was not exactly as I am about to recount, for more than a century has gone by since these events happened, and the skull of the Weakling, as she was known, has weathered snow white at the feet of Saint Ludmila, where she stands benignly smiling in her niche. But the last time I visited her shrine I made my peace with her and asked in advance to be forgiven if I err. The expression carved on her countenance seemed to me tender and reassuring as though she knew that I too love these gentle and generous animals and have tried to do my best by one of them.

It was in the late summer of the year 1823; the herds were still pasturing in the Malbun and *Saminatals,* but the nights were already growing cool so that their days amidst the rich Alpine grass were numbered and the time of their annual descent into the *Rheintal* was not far off.

The setting sun had turned the blue sky a brilliant orange, then soft pink merging to pearl; the plum velvet of night had come out of the east, spangled with stars. The cattle were stamping and lowing softly in the stables nearby. The milking done, the herdsmen and dairymen gathered about the fire which the crisp air made welcome.

Father Polda had walked up from his little chapel in Steg, as was his nightly custom, to sit and talk with the men and their families, for it was mostly under the sun and the stars that he preached, or sought the God that he served.

Alois, the chief herdsman, wrapping his cloak around

him, arose and awakened the echoes with the mournful cry of the ancient Ave he sent aloft each night:

"O-ho! O-ho! A-ve! Ave Maria!"

From the shadowed figures of the herders and dairymen around the fire arose the words and simple melody of the evensong of the herdsmen:

God, the Father, Creator of Heaven and earth,
Give us your blessing, Watch o'er our hearth,
Dearly beloved Mary and your dearly beloved Son,
Let your protecting mantle spread o'er every one,
St. Peter, Thou watchman at Heaven's gate,
Shield us from savage beasts; in Thy hands our fate.

The song swelled louder to include all the saints, Theodul, Rocchus, Wendelin and Veit, Sebastian and St. Cyprian, each of whom had particular duties to protect them from the manifold dangers of the mountains, beasts

of prey, witches, evil spirits, avalanches of rock and snow, the claws of the bear, the fangs of the wolf, the pounce of the lynx, the poisonous breath and the stinging tail of the dragon.

And of course there was Ludmila, *die heilige Notburga,* to whom they sang:

> *Sainted Ludmila, milkmaid without blame,*
> *Make flow rich milk in Holy Maria's name,*
> *Fill every udder; speak thy word,*
> *To grace our beasts and bless our herd . . .*

Father Polda smiled in the darkness. None of the saints had been left out. A big, generous man, he was meticulous with regard to the catalogue of the holy, and even though those whose duty it was to deal with witches and dragons might be thought to have been outmoded by the modernity that was coming to the mountains, he was glad they were still included for politeness' sake and memory of past favors, if nothing else.

Father Polda was a man of great and simple faith who believed in intercession, the force of prayer, and miracles, as opposed to chief herdsman Alois, who though professing belief, was hardheaded and as might be expected of one who lived out in the open and dealt with kine, practical and unsentimental.

Father Polda said: "It has been a good summer—the holy Notburga has done her work well—"

Alois grunted in the dark and lit his long curved pipe until the sparks flew. "There has been plenty of rain, which has made the pasturage rich and the yield good," he said. "It will be better than last year."

"Thanks be to God and Saint Ludmila who has interceded for us."

Alois grunted again. "Saint Ludmila has not been of

much help to Johann Vospelt's weakling. Her yield is far below average. He was cheated when he bought that one."

"Ah," said Father Polda. "The little one with the white muzzle and the ribs showing. It is a pity. Johann needs the money. He has not been well. He has a wife and small child. They spent all their savings to buy the cow."

"She is hardly worth taking to pasture," Alois declared. "She costs more than she can repay. Vospelt would be better off to butcher and sell her. She could not even feed her calf properly. I put it to Schädler's Luzerner champion, who has enough over for a dozen such. There is a beast for you. Butter fat twelve per cent, second yield of cream after the first is skimmed, and cheeses that weigh like stones." He puffed at his pipe a moment and added: "There is no animal in the herd that

can touch her. She is practically certain to lead the procession for the second year for there is hardly more than a week left."

Father Polda did not reply at once, but sat hugging his knees under the black cassock, a huge lump of a man crouched by the fireside looking up into the starry sky behind which were all his friends, and reflecting. Finally he said in a voice that was singularly soft and gentle to emerge from such a giant:

"How unhappy the little Weakling must be. How miserable and wretched. I shall say a prayer for her."

Alois turned and stared at the priest over his pipe. "An animal has no feelings. Pray that Johann Vospelt gets rid of her before she costs him more than she has already."

But Father Polda was right, and Alois was wrong. The little Weakling was most miserable and unhappy indeed. For she was consumed by the hopeless desire to win the right to have her milking stool bedecked with gaily colored ribbons tied to her head at the summer's end.

It is doubtful whether she had dared dream of leading the procession down from the mountainside, wearing the laurel wreath and the big, copper bell, for such was far beyond the capacities of a small, not too well-bred cow.

But that spring, when with the others of the mixed herd owned by the poorer peasants, she had made her slow, toilsome way up the mountain, through the tunnel and into the high pasturage, she was sure that at the very least she could earn a crimson heart or cross for her owner, and what her simple, gentle soul yearned for most dearly was the decoration of the milking stool to wear upon her head.

But the sad truth, as she and the herdsman soon learned, was that she was not very strong and her capacity limited. She was small and thin, and on the whole not to be compared with the huge, sturdy Alpine

90

breeds from whom the milk fairly poured in great, warm, frothy, fragrant streams. Her health was not of the best and there were days when she gave no milk at all.

She was not particularly handsome, lacking the broad head, wide-set eyes, and long, curling eyelashes that gave the others the look of slightly aging beauty queens. She was taupe-colored, but darker and muddier in shade, thin-flanked and high-legged, and differed further from the others by her white muzzle, which made her look even paler and more delicate.

The Weakling tried very hard to be successful, but to little avail. As the weeks passed, she fell further and further behind in her yield. And the more she strained and fretted, the less she seemed to be able to produce.

She took her work seriously, eating heartily, cropping the long, sweet grass indefatigably; she did not take too much exercise, or go climbing to higher pastures which might have disturbed her digestive processes; instead she lay quietly in the shade on hot afternoons, ruminating upon what it would be like to be crowned with the milking stool and cheered and acclaimed by the people. She chewed her cud carefully; she spent long hours thinking the proper thoughts about motherhood and the responsibility of producing milk.

But no matter how hard she tried she could not seem to succeed. When the milker came around to her and pegged his one-legged stool into the clay floor of the stable, he would say: "Ach, it is hardly worth while to bring the pail to you, poor little Weakling." Nevertheless he would milk her out of kindness, for he was a good man, but the result would be no more than a third of a pail, or perhaps even less as the season wore on, with no froth or body to it, but instead a thin, bluish liquid that was deemed fit only to give to the pigs and chickens.

And the little Weakling would often turn her head and eye the slender, hand-turned milking stool, and so great was her yearning that she could almost feel what it would be like to have the seat touch her forehead between her small horns, and hear the rustle of the gaily colored ribbons as they bound it there. For hours afterward, as she stood in her stall, the spot on her brow between the horns would ache with longing for the contact.

The reason that the Weakling so greatly desired the reward of the milking stool was that she was feminine and through no fault of her own had been denied the physique and constitution that would enable her to play the part for which she had been put on earth. She yearned to give lavishly the sweet milk that humans craved for their children and for themselves, she wished to see herself the creator of tubs of creamy butter and round cannon balls of heavy yellow cheeses that would bring wealth to her owner. And female-like, she desired that adornment on the final day which turned the plainest of cows—which she had the misfortune to be—into the most ravishing creature. Capped with the milking stool, garlanded with paper flowers of all colors, beribboned in maroon and blue, she was sure she would please every eye and would arouse the admiration and appreciation of all.

You who believe that animals are dumb and incapable of reason or emotions similar to those experienced by humans will of course continue to do so. I ask you only to think of the yearning and heartache that is the lot of the poor and not-so-favored woman, as she stares through the glass of the shop window at a gay Easter hat, a particularly fetching frock, the sheerest of stockings, or a pair of shoes with little bows that seem to dance all by themselves; lovable articles, desirable articles, magic articles out of her reach since she can neither buy them, nor earn them as a gift, yet things that she knows would transform her in a moment from someone drab and unnoticed, into a sparkling queen, a ravishing beauty that would draw all eyes to her. Or, if not all eyes, then at least a few, and if not a few, then just one pair of eyes, and in the end, the only pair that mattered.

How deep and melancholy is the wish to be beautiful and loved, to be lauded and admired, praised and desired. What power there lies behind the yearning within the feminine heart; what mountains have been moved, armies destroyed, thrones toppled, nations devastated, because of that feminine hunger for something bright, such as a ribbon, a bangle, a diamond, a crown, or the glitter in a man's eye. What civilizations have been built and worlds discovered to satisfy her craving for adornment, to confirm her belief that if only her body were outlined in silks from Cathay and her eyes ringed with kohl from Ind no man could resist her.

Can you really believe that such gigantic forces are engendered and shared only by humans, that this desire to be noticed and admired has not its counterpart in the animal kingdom?

If but the hundredth part of a woman's yearning from time to time for something beautiful to place upon her head, or at her throat, or in her ears, or on her back was what the little Weakling was experiencing in her desire to be distinguished as the most successful and desirable of her sex, then she was still the most miserable, unhappiest and most forlorn of all cows. For as the summer drew to a close she knew that her chances of succeeding were hopeless and that perhaps never in all her life would she taste that sweetness in the hour of triumph that was to come to her more fortunate companions.

It did not embitter her, however. It only made her sad, and increased the power of her yearning. She continued to see herself longingly, udders distended to aching with rich, creamy milk, and hear the welcome sound as it frothed into the pail until it filled to overflowing. And then she would feel the milk stool upon her head.

But by the end of the summer, the little Weakling was even more unprepossessing. She was gaunt, ungainly, her gait awkward, her udders slack and all but dry. Only her eyes preserved their luminosity and more than ever were filled with perpetual sadness.

One evening, when the herds had been grazing in the lower Samina Valley and were returning to Malbun for the night, Father Polda came forth from his little chapel and joined leathery old Alois, the chief herdsman, for his evening walk, and side by side they marched up the path alongside the mountain torrent, conversing to the peaceful rushing of the water that mingled with the musical jangling and tonkling of the deep-toned bells around the necks of the cattle.

They discussed the forthcoming descent, the bounty of the year, the prices that would be fetched in the market by the season's yield of butter and cheese, which would mean prosperity for all the valley, all except poor farmer Vospelt whose weakling cow had yielded so little.

Thus the subject of the Weakling was revived, and Father Polda noted that they had already passed the shrine of Saint Ludmila in her niche in the rock. He had meant in passing to say another prayer for the little cow, to ask the holy Notburga to intercede not only for the unfortunate animal, but also for farmer Vospelt, who needed the money so much for his family. He realized that it was too late for such intercession to do much good unless by a miracle, but he also believed there was no harm in trying.

They heard a sharp barking, and as they looked back they saw that Alois' work dog was yapping at the heels of

94

the poor Weakling, who as usual had fallen behind the others in the ascent, and was making no attempt to continue, nor was she paying the slightest attention to the animal baying at her heels.

Instead, as the two men gazed they could see that she had turned broadside to the path and was standing staring across the white-frothed torrent to the figure of Saint Ludmila, or rather the doll-like image of her that had been created by Anton the woodcarver of Steg, many, many years ago.

Since there were no pictures extant of *die heilige Notburga,* the woodcarver had taken the expression he had carved on her face from his own heart, one that had likewise loved the gentle members of the Creator's animal kingdom to whom He had assigned the task of extending the bounty of their motherhood to man.

Thus her smile was warm, tender, loving and yet infinitely pitying too, and invited a similar expression to the lips of all those who passed, and many, seeing her, would murmur: "Dear Saint Ludmila, holy Notburga, give the sweetness and warmth of your protection to me likewise."

And so the two men saw Saint Ludmila smiling down at the little Weakling, and the Weakling standing there, unmindful of the dog that other times would have terrified her, and gazing up at the holy Notburga, her eyes filled with hopeless and gentle pleading as well as the infinite longing and love that filled her being.

Alois said to Father Polda: "Your little Weakling has grown impatient, waiting for your prayers." He laughed good-humoredly. "It looks as though she has decided to ask Saint Ludmila to intercede for her herself. She's gone one ahead of you, Father."

But Father Polda was not amused, for the saints and

95

prayer were something he took seriously, and he rebuked Alois angrily for levity verging on blasphemy.

"The Heavenly Father takes all animals both great and small under His shelter," he said, "but He did not give them the capacity to pray. That is for us to do for them, else He would have bestowed upon them the power of speech. You should not joke about such matters."

Alois, who for all of his hardheadedness was a believer and who also was a little afraid of Father Polda, mumbled in his square brown beard that he had not meant to give offense, whistled to his dog, and they turned up the mountain path again and soon the little Weakling came trotting after.

But this time it was perhaps Father Polda who was wrong, and the herdsman who could have been right.

For a prayer need not be a rhetorical address, or an itemized petition, or lips moved soundlessly inside a

cathedral, or even words spoken into the air. A prayer may be a wordless inner longing, a sudden outpouring of love, a yearning within the soul to be for a moment united with the infinite and the good, a humbleness that needs no abasement or speech to express it, a cry in the darkness for help when all seems lost, a song, a poem, a kind deed, a reaching for beauty, or the strong, quiet inner reaffirmation of faith.

A prayer in fact can be anything that is created of God that turns to God.

The little Weakling did not know that she was praying when she paused on the path, her eyes caught by the bright object shining from the niche in the rock. She was aware of nothing but the sadness in her being and unutterable longing to pour forth her love in the shape of milk and thereafter to satisfy her yearning for the beribboned milking stool to be given her.

There is no way she could express or articulate this hunger, but it was particularly strong that evening as she returned with her udders almost flat. The figure in the rocks caught her gentle eyes. She turned to it in the moment when it seemed as though her unhappiness and shame would overwhelm her, and she stood there trembling with the intensity of her desire to be as all the others and know the joy of giving as well as receiving.

And so, in a sense she made a prayer, and having done so, it existed; it was loosed. It was directed at the figure of the one whose love and duty called for her to intercede at the throne; and as with all prayers that arise from the sincere and loving heart, it was both heard and felt, in the far corners of the universe. For whereas evil has no power to extend beyond its own radius, the living trust of a child, or the whispered confession of a sincere and tender heart can alter the stars in their courses. The gentle plea of a maid, asking for a bit of ribbon or cambric for her hair rings as loudly as the Cardinal's Latin in the outer spaces of time or thought, whence destiny is directed.

Surely you do not think that God is angry at the desires of His creatures to win affection and appear beautiful and desirable in the eyes of others. For He Himself loves beauty since He created so much of it on the face of the earth in both man and beast. And who but He caused the peasants of Liechtenstein to think of something so gay, innocent, and charming as the wreathing of their beasts with laurel and garlands when the year's harvest was garnered, and crowning them with the insignia of their gentle serviture, the milking stool?

It was the next day that Alois decided to take the cattle for the last time up to the highest pasture just below the *Sareiserjoch* where the green slopes are watered by crystal springs that gush from the rocks.

As the herdsmen and dogs marshaled the beasts for the climb, for the pasture lay a thousand feet above them, his eyes fell upon the Weakling, and he found himself torn between a mixture of annoyance as he remembered the reproof of Father Polda administered the night before, and pity for the animal that was so thin and generally ill-favored. He genuinely loved the animals that had been entrusted to his care, and watched over them.

As he looked, he thought of the long climb and the poor condition of the beast, as well as the plight of farmer Vospelt should the animal die on the heights and have to be sold for what her hide would bring for leather. And, too, there was the celebration and descent to be thought of, now less than a week away. It would be foolish to take chances, for it was a part of the custom that if during the season there was an accident, or one of the animals died, the ceremony of the milking stools, the ribbons, and the gay decorations was dispensed with for that year.

He said to the herdsmen: "Let her be, the little Weakling. She is not worth taking to the high pasture now. She is out of the running for the prizes, anyway. Let her remain down here where she will be safe."

And then he called to his youngest daughter, aged seven, who was playing nearby, and who too was named Ludmila after *die heilige Notburga:* "Ludmila, come here. Look after the little Weakling today and see that she comes to no harm. She is to remain behind. Do not let her stray out of your sight and see that she is back in the stall by sundown."

And with that the dogs were set to work, the herdsmen cried "Heuh!" Beasts and herders set off up the mountain.

Little Ludmila had brown legs and arms, a brown face, and brown hair, but her eyes were as blue as the cornflowers and wild delphinium that grew in the mountain meadows. She went at once and put her arms around the little Weakling's neck and laid her cheek next its soft, white muzzle, and then taking hold of the end of her halter marched off with her, with the Weakling following on docilely behind, her bell giving off a musical clang with every other step she took.

Some children would have been upset at having their day's play disturbed by such a peremptory order to take charge of a derelict animal that was not good for much of anything, but Ludmila was pleased, for she had for a long time wished to go into the dark glen at the foot of the *Bettlerjoch* a short distance away to look for elves which she was sure lived there.

She was afraid to go alone, for there might be other things there as well, such as witches, or little hairy wild men with peaked hats and long noses and ears who hid behind rocks with only the tips of their ears and the points of their hats showing, or even perhaps a small dragon.

But with the little cow along as her companion, her bronze bell tonkling loudly to frighten away any evil spirits, and her warm and comforting presence there and the halter to cling to, Ludmila felt no fear at all, and soon child and beast were lost to sight as they left the little community at Malbun and chose the path toward Gritsch and the deep wild glen at the bottom of the *Bettlerjoch*.

The sturdy brown legs took the child over a winding Alpine road that soon plunged into a dark pine forest. Shortly they came to a spot where the path split in two and on the right descended sharply into a dark and rocky ravine where fallen trees were tumbled like jackstraws and the boulders lay strewn about as though flung by a giant hand.

This was the mysterious ravine of the *Bettlerjoch*. Mounting, it grew wilder and more tumultuous until it reached to that mass of granite pillars and monoliths with the curiously human forms which legend said were the Butter Beggars, those wandering friars who came over the pass known as the *Nenzinger Himmel* through the *Joch* to the high pasturage to beg for butter for the cold winter days to come and in return bestowed their blessings on herdsmen and herds and prayed for them, and who one day were overtaken by a terrible storm and their forms frozen there forever.

But descending, the terrain grew less wild; there were little patches of grass and meadow with many herbs and wildflowers that seemed to flourish nowhere else.

For a moment, Ludmila hesitated to enter this unfamiliar territory, but the Weakling's bell jangled reassuringly, and when the animal also gave forth a soft "Moo," she hesitated no longer, and taking the halter

101

once more in her chubby fist entered the side of the ravine by the right-hand path and descended to the glen below.

The elves were there in the form of splinters of sunlight flashing from the quartz in the granite, or filtering through the greenery, dappling the leaves of the trees, and the child pursued them deeper and deeper into the ravine until they vanished in the darkness of tumbled rock or cave, or dense pines where the sun no longer penetrated.

Soon they came to a kind of glade opening out from the lower part of the glen through a rocky path. Here the land leveled for a space, a rushing brook quietened, as it meandered through this hidden meadow ringed with trees, and rich with sweet-smelling herbs and flowers, yellow blossoms with broad leaves amongst ferns, lichens, and algae, arenarias and saxifrages growing amidst dark grasses.

The little Weakling commenced to feed contentedly, shaded by a gigantic oak tree that spread its branches in huge circumference and beneath which, amidst a scattering of sweet acorns, the flowering herbs and weeds grew in thick profusion.

Comforted by the sound of the bell about the neck of the Weakling and her eager munching, Ludmila explored the boundaries of what was obviously a magic circle on enchanted ground; watching the long blue shadows of the trout as they sunned themselves in the brook, discovering a gray badger with shining eyes working at the mouth of his hole, startling a young deer, coming upon a whole family of little hamsters feeding on acorns and noting hundreds of tiny green-breasted finches and blue-headed tits flitting through the branches of the trees and peering out from behind the leaves.

And in this manner, with the Weakling feeding placidly, and the child, herself turned into the very kind of woodland and mountain elf she sought, playing in and about the beautiful glen and all its wild things, time passed. The shadows grew longer, the air cooler, and the sun began to dip toward the jagged rim of the mountain peaks visible through the trunks of the tall pines, and her instincts told Ludmila that it was time to return home.

But the day had been long, exciting, and strenuous, and she was both hungry and thirsty. And since she was a

herdsman's daughter, Ludmila knew both where and how to provide herself with food and went directly to the source.

She secured the Weakling's trailing halter and led her to a sapling where she made her fast. Then seating herself at the hind quarters she took one of the soft teats, directed it at her mouth, closed her eyes, and began to milk.

At the touch of the little hands, so different from the rough, strong, horny palms of the herdsmen, it seemed as

though a shudder ran through the Weakling. For the first moment as the child tugged, first at one then at another, there was no response. Not even the thin bluish trickle rewarded her efforts. But again, the shudder shook the animal and she stood there, her feet spread apart, trembling as though in the grip of a mountain chill. All her pent-up anguish seemed to find expression in the single cry, half a moo and half a moan that came from her throat and echoed from the pillars that represented the frozen friars of the *Bettlerjoch* above and went sighing off into the peaks. And then her milk began to flow.

A few drops at first, then a trickle, then a stream, and soon, a warm, rich, fragrant jet shot into the mouth of Ludmila, causing her to gurgle and laugh with surprise, pleasure, and satisfaction, a sound which surely to the Weakling must have been the most beautiful she had ever heard. At last, she was giving, as God had intended her to do.

The child drank until she could hold no more, and thereafter led the Weakling to the stream to let her refresh herself, and then taking her in tow, set off through the rocky path that led from the enchanted meadow, through the glen and up the ravine on the homeward path. And for the first time since she had matured, the Weakling, her heart filled with joy, felt the ache of plenitude in her udders and the need to be further relieved of the gift she carried there.

That night, when the herdsmen, accompanying their proud, sleek cattle, returned from the high pasturage by the *Sareiserjoch,* to the huts and stables just below the slopes of Malbun and the milkers took to their metal pails and one-legged milking stools, the miracle of Saint Ludmila, the holy milkmaid Notburga, began.

The Weakling was already standing in her stall,

emitting low moos, of pleasurable pain, when from force of habit the milker arrived at her side, set stool and pail, seized the nearest teat and squeezed perfunctorily, for he was weary from serving the heavy yielders and was grateful that the day was drawing to a close.

But the first sound of the powerful stream of milk landing with a clang at the bottom of the pail awoke him and caused him to cry out in amazement, as by the light of the lantern that hung from the roof of the milking shed he saw the distended skin of the swollen udders bearing such a burden as he had never encountered before in this unfortunate little animal.

He remembered the poor quality of her yield and still by habit, milked on, but when the pail was half full, his cry arose over the stamping of the hoofs in the shed, the switching of tails, and the rush of the milk—"Hola, Alois! Hola there, send for Alois. The Chief herdsman is to come here at once to see what has happened."

Alois came and stared likewise, for now the pail was three-quarters filled with creamy liquid topped by foaming bubbles of fatty froth, as rich as any that ever came from the big Swiss champions in the herd.

The pail was filled to overflowing, another was placed beside her, once again the powerful jet of milk clanged against the empty sides, the liquid, warm and pungent, began to foam as it climbed up the pail. The other milkers and herders crowded into the shed as word spread of the astonishing thing that was happening to the little Weakling, and a moment later there was a movement in the throng and the huge bulk of Father Polda bent over to pass through the door.

He glanced at the full milk pail, the second filling beneath the fingers of the milker, the color of the fluid and the oily quality of the froth that topped it, and crossed himself.

"Holy Saint Ludmila, Holy Notburga!" he cried. "It is a miracle!" for he wished it so.

Alois grunted as was his custom when he was about to become hardheaded and did not wish to admit something, especially to the priest. "Some of these sickly ones come into milk late sometimes. We will see. The milk may be sour, or deficient. Wait until it has been separated."

At last the udders were emptied, the second pail was nearly filled and taken away to be tested for fat and butter content, darkness fell, supper was eaten and the men gathered about the fire, and once again the Mountain Ave rang out—"O-ho! O-ho! A-ve! Ave Maria!"—when the herdsman whose duty it was to watch by night by the stables came running into the circle, pale and out of breath:

"Alois! Father Polda! The one with the white muzzle, the little Weakling that was milked last tonight! I heard her complaining and went with the lantern to look. Her udders are filled again. She must be milked at once. Come and see if you do not believe me."

It was true. Scarce three hours had passed, but the milk sacs were again distended and heavy with their burden. A milker was hastily summoned, and again the rich, yellowish liquid thundered into the pail; once more a second receptacle had to be fetched to hold the yield.

Father Polda crossed himself again and cried: "Holy Saint Ludmila, a miracle, a miracle indeed. Well, Alois, what have you to say now?"

But the chief herdsman did not reply. He only stared bewildered at this amazing thing, though it was noted that he crossed himself likewise.

In the meantime, a layer of heavy, yellowish cream, six inches deep, and so thick that one might have stood up a spoon in it without its falling over had gathered at the top of the first two pails, that the little Weakling had filled earlier. Here was butter fat and a wealth of it such as had not been seen produced on the high pasturage within living memory.

All through the night and the next day and the next after that it went on. Replenishing herself, it seemed, with no more than copious draughts from buckets of water, the Weakling continued to give of her so long withheld riches every three or four hours, wearing out relays of milkmen whose arms became heavy and fingers cramped as they worked to relieve her of her sudden treasure.

Word began to travel of the miracle that was taking place and mountaineers and woodcutters, keepers of hospices and charcoal burners from the neighboring peaks and valleys came over to the milking shed in Malbun to see for themselves, and soon there was no room inside for everyone and so the gentle little creature with the white muzzle, thin flanks, and tender eyes was moved out into the open where all could see her and watch the fabulous torrents of milk that poured from her.

She stood there then in a kind of daze, wrapped in the glory of bestowing and the fulfillment of that part of her yearning that had to do with udders filled with life-giving food and drink that now was hers to share.

On the third day, the head dairyman came bustling from the cheese and butter factories next the milking shed in a state of excitement, shouting; "One more pail, and the little one will win best of her group. She already has heart and cross won and needs only another gallon to catch up and surpass the best of her herd. It does not seem possible."

It was Father Polda who replied: "Oh, yes. With a miracle, everything is possible, when there is faith in

goodness and belief in the Creator whose will has called forth greater things even than this. She may even, who knows, be the first cow through the tunnel at Steg, bearing the bell and garland of victory—"

But here Alois and his hard head were heard from. "That cannot be," he said. "Schädler's Luzerner has won the right of first cow by many tens of pounds. It will be impossible for the little one to overtake her. For the woodcutter who has just arrived over the *Bettlerjoch* tells me that the first snow has appeared on the *Panülerkopf* and the *Hornspitz.* Tomorrow we return to the valley."

Father Polda sighed and said nothing, for the word of the chief herdsman in all things pertaining to the herds entrusted to his care was law, and no one dared question his commands. But it being Father Polda's first personal miracle, he wished to see it taken to a climax.

At that, the Weakling barely made the final pail that was needed to give her the honor of the milking stool. For the great and miraculous flow seemed at last to come to an end, and it was all the milkers could do to wring the last drops from her fabulous udders. Yet achieve it she did though the effort left her weak and spent and she was led on tottery legs to the shelter of the stall, fed and watered and allowed to rest for the great event of the descent the following day.

And thus it was that the poor little Weakling, whose hopes of realizing her desire to be decorated with her milking stool had seemed so utterly impossible of fulfillment, was led forth the next day, cleaned, washed, brushed, so that thin and emaciated as she was, her dun-colored hide glistened. Hoofs and horns were polished until they sparkled in the sunlight and at last came the moment when she felt the seat of the milking stool pressed against her head between the horns by rough but kind hands and lashed there with gaily-colored ribbons.

Streamers were fastened to the stool's leg, paper flowers and cockades attached to her headstall and about her ears; garlands of flowers hung about her neck. Small-boned, and lacking the stalwart maturity of the older animals, her head graced by the decorations, her sweetness of expression gave her the air of a young girl going to her first ball. She became suddenly innocently beautiful and heart-warmingly radiant.

Now, word of the event that had taken place on the high pasturage had also reached to the village of Vaduz, which heard the rumor of how the poor peasant Vospelt's animal that had been last in yield of dairy products had in the final three days, by the intervention of Saint Ludmila, poured forth a miraculous stream of milk.

Outside the tunnel, the crowds gathered to wait in

twice the number they ever had before. They came up from Vaduz, the capital, and Schaan and Triesen, Mäls and Balzers, Nendeln and Eschen, to climb the lofty Triesenberg on foot and take up their position of vantage at Gnalp, to see for themselves whether there was any truth in the strange marvel that had been reported from the fastnesses of the high pasturage.

Because it might be an ecclesiastical affair, if true, the Herr Canonicus Josef from the big church in Vaduz was there with lesser members of the clergy from the vicinity, and since if it were actually so it would redound to the eternal credit of Liechtenstein, a member of the ruling family from the *Schloss* below arrived, incognito of course.

Spontaneously, and without invitation, the brass band from Schaanwald appeared, the *Männerchor* from Planken and the girl singers from Mauren and Ruggell. The *Bürgermeister* of Vaduz came in his robes as did the president of the council and the ministers from Switzerland and Austria.

Naturally the attraction was likewise to see which would be the lead cow this year, but behind the huge turnout lay excitement of perhaps witnessing a marvel of some sort. It could of course hardly be true that the poor, sickly little animal they all remembered as belonging to peasant Vospelt, and which few had deemed worth even sending up to the high pasturage, could really have won a prize, much less the decoration of the milking stool, but if there was any truth in the rumors, they were all there and prepared to see.

In Malbun the cavalcade was ready for the descent. Cattle, horses, men, women, children, dogs, all were groomed and dressed in their best and decorated in every manner possible to mark the wonderful occasion.

An hour after sunup the procession gathered on the

113

meadow nearby the little community of huts, sheds, and barns where they had all lived together during the long summer and the doors and windows of which were now boarded up.

Father Polda stood upon a drinking trough and blessed them, as was his custom, and sent up a prayer of gratitude to Saint Ludmila for the miracle she had created for them. Then with cries from the herders, the cracking of whips, the barking of dogs, and the gay singing of the women and children, they started down the Malbun, next the roaring torrent to Steg.

First in the line, the silver clapper of the great brazen bell about her neck booming her approach, came Schädler's great champion Luzerner, winning beast the second year in succession, milk stool worn proudly as one who was used to such articles borne upon her head. Then came Gruber's Frisian, and Wohlmayr's Züricher champion in second and third place, followed by several others that had ranked high. Thereafter proudly heading the last division of the mixed herd belonging to many poor peasants tottered the little Weakling with her gay decorations and sweet exalted expression, looking like a mixture of half cocotte, half angel. At her head marched Ludmila, cornflowers the color of her eyes braided in her brown hair. At her side walked Father Polda.

The three came eventually to the shrine of the holy Notburga by the torrent Malbun, and here they paused and turned to her as though by mutual understanding and consent, the huge man in the black cassock, the brown, barelegged child, and the Weakling. No word was spoken. Ludmila had her arm about the neck of the animal, and together they stood by the wooden rail that guarded people from falling into the stream and looked across the silvery waters to the figure in the niche, the sweet little doll with the tender expression on her carved and painted countenance.

On the child's face was wonder. In the eyes of the Weakling was deathless love. On the lips of Father Polda was a prayer. There they remained thus for a long time, so long that chief herdsman Alois returned to see what was holding up the procession and thus he found them.

When her father came up, the child suddenly left the little cow and ran to him, put her arms around his neck and began to cry, causing him to say: "Now now, Ludmila, what is the matter? Why are you crying?"

"Because of my little cow who is so beautiful. Saint Ludmila wishes her to lead all the others."

The chief herdsman was much less hardheaded when it came to his daughter and he smiled at her and said: "She does, does she? And how would you know this?"

Ludmila stopped crying and took her father's hand and led him to the rail, looked across to Saint Ludmila and replied: "Because she spoke to me, and *told me so*. Please, papa, let her be the first."

Alois looked from his daughter to the Weakling, to Father Polda standing at her side and said harshly: "What is this nonsense? Have you been putting ideas into the child's head? What does she mean the saint spoke to her? Did you hear anything?"

Father Polda smiled, and gently shook his head. "I heard nothing," he said. "But sometimes little children can hear things that we cannot."

For a moment the big, bearded herdsman stood there staring at the statue. Then he picked up the child on his arm and strode away down the path. Man and beast followed.

But at Steg, the last stopping place before they moved down the *Saminatal* and entered the rock tunnel to emerge into the world beyond, chief herdsman Alois

115

gave brief and sharp orders; two herdsmen came to the rear of the procession and led the little Weakling forward to the head of the line. There, while many looked aghast and all stared in utter amazement, they took the great black-silver star and heart-studded bell with the polished black leather collar from the leading cow and hung it about her neck. They likewise removed the crown of laurel leaves from the noble brow of the Luzerner champion and draped it about the head of the Weakling, for whom it was too big, and therefore fell slightly askew, giving her an even more coquettish air. In her emaciated state from the great effort she had made, the weight of the big bell was almost more than she could carry. Then the halter lead was put into the hands of Ludmila. The Weakling staggered forward and the two, now at the head of the procession, led the way down the road into tunnel.

It was wrong and arbitrary, what Alois did, for Schädler's big Luzerner had fairly won the right to lead them all home a second year and one voice from the crowd protested, "Halloo there, Mr. Chief Herdsman, what is going on? Everyone knows that Schädler's animal is the winner."

But with a terrible frown, Alois cried, "Quiet! Saint Ludmila herself has commanded that the Weakling lead us home!" And thereafter none dared dispute his decision.

Soon the dense crowds lining both sides of the road on the other side of the tunnel heard the irregular booming of the big cowbell around the neck of the approaching leader. It would ring, then stop, then ring faintly, again louder as it approached, more faintly again, and once it jangled harshly as though the bearer had fallen.

Murmurs and shivers of excitement ran through the

crowd. Louder and louder sounded the great bell and steadier now. The moment was at hand.

Out of the mouth of the tunnel stepped a brown elf with cornflowers the color of her eyes braided through her brown hair, leading a small thin cow with a white muzzle, belled, crowned, and garlanded. For a moment they stood blinking in the sunlight. Then a great shout went up from the throng, almost like a hosanna, a cheer and a cry and a greeting and a prayer all in one. Men waved their hats and shouted, women wept and sobbed.

It was true. The miracle had taken place, for there was the evidence before their very eyes. Not only had the poor despised Weakling won the right to wear her milk stool, but the champion's laurels and winner's position, the prize of best cow of the year had come to her. Only a saint could have made this possible.

Then the brass band struck up the national anthem of Liechtenstein, the *Männerchor* burst into song as did the *Sängerbund* of girls from Mauren and Ruggell, and the women's choir from Triesenberg.

His Highness, the member of the Royal family, dropped his incognito and stepped forward to pin a glittering medal, the Royal Double Eagle First Class to the Weakling's collar and pick up the child Ludmila in his arms and kiss her. Herr Canonicus Josef suddenly knelt in the road, followed by the other members of the clergy, and struck up an "Alleluia" and the next moment men, women, and children in the huge throng of welcomers likewise went to their knees, singing and giving thanks to Him and those on High from Whom all miracles and blessings flow.

And so, her greatest desire and dream of glory came to realization, the little Weakling, burdened with the earthly prizes awarded to her by Heavenly dispensation, looked

out upon this strange scene, the towering mountains opposite, the blue thread of the Rhine in the valley far below, the people in their Sunday best kneeling in the road, the black-robed priests, the stately figure of His Highness, and her eyes were gentle and swimming, filled with love and happiness, that all this which she had so much desired had in the end happened to her, and that before her final moment she had been privileged to give.

For the effort and the strain of the last three days had been too much for her, and with that sure instinct of animals, she knew she was looking upon the sunshine and the kindly people whom it had been her duty to feed for the last time. And she was content.

The big bell boomed again. The sun glittered from the golden medal at her collar. Child and animal started forward again down the mountain followed by the gay and colorful procession of the annual return from the high pasturage.

There is not much more to the story. Worn out by her efforts, the little Weakling passed away in the valley before sundown that evening. Yet strangely it did not put a damper on the celebration, or the happiness of the people at having been singled out for the execution of a miracle in their midst. They and the Canonicus saw it quite simply as the logical extension of the miracle whereby, having performed it and demonstrated her love and power via the Weakling, Saint Ludmila, the holy Notburga had taken the little animal to her as her reward and she would henceforth graze peacefully and happily in the Heavenly pastures close to the side of her living friend and patron. And it is for this reason that the skull and horns of the Weakling were bestowed on the shrine of the saint.

The butter and cheese made from the miraculous milk of the Weakling brought their weight in gold and never again would the poor peasant Vospelt or his family want for anything.

Only one thing more remains to be told.

A week later, chief herdsman Alois suddenly appeared at Steg in the Samina Valley with the child Ludmila at his side and sought out Father Polda in the tiny chapel.

"Come," he said to the priest. "Come with us."

They walked, all three in silence up the path again past the shrine in the rocks to which Alois did not so much as vouchsafe a glance now, until they came to the deserted huts and barns on the Malbun slope. Here it was that the little Ludmila at her father's behest took over the leadership, and with the sure orientation of the mountain child, led them up the path to the *Bettlerjoch.* As she had once before, she branched off from the main dark and fearsome ravine downward toward the glen of the elves, and thence through the rock path to the magic circle in the enchanted meadow peaceful in the morning sun with only the sound of birds in the great oak, the rustling of small animals in the underbrush, and the gentle murmur of the stream resting before it resumed its plunge below.

Alois now roved about this meadow, his eyes on the ground; he went to the brook, came back, knelt near the oak tree and examined the ground, arose and went to the opposite side and did the same. And as he searched, his dark, bearded face lit up with satisfaction and at last he came over and faced Father Polda.

"Well," asked the priest. "Why have you brought me here? What is it you have discovered?"

"This," said Alois. "Look there. Do you recognize that little weed with the yellow flower and the broad leaf?"

Father Polda gazed down at the plant that seemed to be growing in unusual profusion all about them. "It is the *Alchemilla*," he replied. "The *Mutterkraut*."

"Yes," said the herdsman. "Have you ever seen so much at one time?"

The priest shook his head. "No. It is most unusual."

"Ah! Then come here and look. Here under the oak tree, it grows almost solid. But see where it has been cropped, and the hoofmarks of an animal. Round and about this tree it has been eaten away—"

"Well—?" said the priest.

Alois threw him a look of triumph. "It was here that Ludmila came that day with the little Weakling when I refused to take her along to the high pasture. Those are her hoofmarks. The little one in a few hours found and consumed more *Mutterkraut* than most Alpine cattle would in a lifetime. The whole day she grazed upon the *Alchemilla*. In the evening, her milk glands violently stimulated, she started to give milk." He smiled in triumph again and looked the priest in the eye. "There is your miracle of Saint Ludmila for you. It is explained as I always knew it must be."

The priest remained silent and his eyes were bent to the ground where the hoofprints of the little Weakling were still plain to be seen as well as the close-to-the-ground cropped ends of many of the *Alchemilla* plants which somehow had flourished in this secluded place.

"Well," asked the chief herdsman, "what have you to say?"

The priest looked up, but his brow was unclouded and his eyes untroubled and clear. "Yes," he said finally. "You are right. The miracle is indeed explained for all of those for whom the miracles must always be explained lest humans be forced to confess that they are not as important as they believe themselves to be."

Alois said: "You admit then that now we know why all of a sudden the Weakling gave so much milk and of such high content that in the end it was like giving her heart's blood and strength and it killed her?"

A little smile now played about the lips of the big priest. "That is correct," he said. "Now we know why the little one suddenly gave so much milk. Ah, yes, now we know everything."

"Eh?" said Alois, suspiciously, struck by something in the tone of the priest. "What do you mean by everything?"

"Oh," replied Father Polda, still smiling, "all the other miracles which you will explain to me—what made you say that day the little Weakling was praying at the shrine of Saint Ludmila, what was it that led you to decide against taking the animal to the high pasturage that day, how you came to entrust her to little Ludmila's care—also of course how the child came to wander here to this deserted glen where no ordinary child would venture alone, and how together they discovered this marvelous patch of *Mutterkraut*—and finally of course the greatest wonder of all, what made you decide in one moment to listen to your child, go against the records and at the last minute name the Weakling champion cow and leader of the descent into the valley, thus setting the final stamp and seal on the miracle in which you do not believe."

He paused and offered his hand to the child who took it confidingly. "Come," he said, "let us go from here." He turned to Alois still smiling gently, "But there will be time for those explanations later—"

He walked slowly hand in hand with Ludmila back the way they had come through the rocky defile. Behind them Alois walked silently, his head bent toward the ground as one in deep thought. . . .